H E N R Y
CALVIN

"A delightful book! A romp through Normandy with an unhysterical heroine, whose good sense merely compounds her jeopardy, and a hero, wry and romantic and very French."

—Dorothy Salisbury Davis

"This book brought that peculiar content which only comes with a good story, well loved and well told by a witful author."

—Dorothy B. Hughes

"Henry Calvin...writes with such deceptive simplicity and directness; to me that is storytelling at its best."

—Doris Miles Disney

IT'S DIFFERENT ABROAD

HENRY CALVIN

PERENNIAL LIBRARY

Harper & Row, Publishers

New York, Cambridge, Philadelphia, San Francisco
London, Mexico City, São Paulo, Sydney

A hardcover edition of this book was published by Harper & Row, Publishers, Inc.

IT'S DIFFERENT ABROAD. Copyright © 1963 by Henry Calvin. All rights reserved. Printed in the United States of America. No part of this book may be used or reproduced in any manner whatsoever without written permission except in the case of brief quotations embodied in critical articles and reviews. For information address Harper & Row, Publishers, Inc., 10 East 53rd Street, New York, N.Y. 10022.

First PERENNIAL LIBRARY edition published 1983.

LIBRARY OF CONGRESS CATALOG CARD NUMBER: 82-48241

ISBN: 0-06-080640-0

83 84 85 10 9 8 7 6 5 4 3 2 1

1 *WHEN THE LITTLE RED CAR FINALLY STOOD ON*
the tarmac at Le Touquet, she felt like laughing aloud. The
fact of being on French soil, of being at last abroad, was delight enough. Since she had a habit of examining her impulses,
she suspected that her elation might be partly the result of
fatigue, a kind of intoxication of exhaustion. She had driven
the little car five hundred miles, mostly through the night, in
order to reach the south coast and the airport, and she knew
this was foolish.

Her name was Helen McLeish; spinster ("of this parish?"
she thought—no, "of no fixed abode" sounded less stuffy. She
smiled at her foolishness). Hair brown, eyes brown. Age
thirty-four. And free, she reminded herself. Free. On the long
trip through England she had even put her foot down and
watched the speedometer needle flickering round seventy.
Reckless speed, even for a few moments at a time, was a
symbolic act of defiance. She was in love with the little car,
absolutely besotted. She would cheerfully have driven nonstop
to China.

In fact, she was in love with everything at that moment. The
sun was higher in the sky than it ever rose at home, and this
surprised and delighted her. She had never imagined that
five hundred mere miles of latitude could make such a dif-

1

ference. The most banal things were a joy to her eyes. A notice proclaiming SORTIE, the new smell of a foreign country, the bleached and faded blue overalls of workmen, the sharp glaring outlines of buildings in the sun. She had never been out of Scotland in her life, but she had nursed a lifelong love affair with the idea of France too, and the first sight of her beloved was exactly as she had imagined it. It was strange, but not strange, like the recognition of a place familiar in a dream. The knowledge of her sheer distance from home was a physical sensation. Having smiled once, she composed her face and kept the laughter inside. She was not, after all, an adolescent romantic fool, but a grown woman, humdrum but mature, even sophisticated.

"Anything to declare?" the customs man asked. He had a black mustache and a surly expression.

"Rien que mes espoirs," she said gravely. "Nothing but my hopes." His face didn't flicker.

"Take good care of them, mademoiselle," he muttered. She loved him. She started her little car and drove carefully out into France.

Berry and Laurent picked her up at this point and slid into the traffic behind her. Laurent, the shorter one, was at the wheel of their big Citroën, which was black, ten years old and utterly anonymous.

"Are you sure that's her?" Berry asked him. "She doesn't look too old."

"She's the one," said Laurent.

"She doesn't look too old."

"She's too old for you," Laurent burst out. "Keep away from her. All we want is the car."

"She doesn't look too old," Berry repeated happily, because

2

he knew it annoyed Laurent. "A woman of a certain age can be very rewarding."

"Good," Laurent told him. "You have her. I'll take the car. A fair carve-up. Now shut up."

Berry smiled sleepily to himself, took a comb from his shirt pocket and ran it through his fair hair. Berry was a beautiful young man.

"Damn," said Laurent, "she's going to stop."

Berry became at once alert. The little red car ahead was slowing down beside a café.

"Maybe she's meeting them here," he said, and Laurent told him not to be a fool.

"All right, I'm a fool!" Berry was no longer sleepy or amused. "If the bitch meets them here, we've had it."

Laurent turned to him and sneered.

"O.K., handsome," he said, "what would you like to do—knock her down in the street before she can talk to anybody? Here, in this street?"

Berry was already opening the door.

"Let me out," he said. "I'll keep an eye on her. Just stay here and be ready to follow."

He was out of the car before Laurent could stop him. Laurent breathed through his nose and gripped the wheel tight. Berry was a useful man, but he had no brain of any kind. His impulses were those of a greedy, ruthless child.

Helen had been driving with infinite care on the right side of the road, a thing she had rehearsed constantly in her dreams but was still terrified of forgetting. The intoxication was still with her, but she could also feel the premonition of a headache. Fatigue and sunshine. She had a sudden lust for a cup of tea. The proverbial British tourist, she thought wryly. Ten

3

seconds on French soil and howling for tea. Nevertheless, she wanted a cup of tea, and she stopped carefully at the first likely-looking café (WE SERVE HAM AND EGGS). She hadn't closed the door when a shadow fell on her and a man's voice said, "Mademoiselle . . ."

She turned to see a tall, beautiful young man flashing two rows of white teeth in a honey-tanned face.

"You drive . . . west?" The young man waved one hand, with infinite grace, in the direction of America.

"No," Helen said firmly. "I go to drink tea."

"Ah, very good, the tea. And after, you drive west?"

Tales of a Traveling Spinster, she thought—ten minutes in France and I was accosted by a man. Such a handsome man too, mm, muscle and shoulders and everything, even French charm, I swear it.

Berry was smiling humorously at her.

"Ah, not to worry, mademoiselle," he assured her. "I am most respectable. Perhaps mademoiselle give me lift? To . . . Saint-Lunquire, only. Simple." A touch of genius, Berry thought. The story and the smile together were irresistible, he was on.

He was not on. Helen was shaking her head and quite unimpressed.

"No," she said, "I give lifts only to small children and old men with broken legs."

"Ah, I am no trouble, mademoiselle." Berry laid a hand on her arm to detain her. They always said no at first. Helen was a firm and practical woman, amused at her own visions of seduction, rape, robbery, murder. The beautiful young man was only a hitchhiker. On the other hand, when you came to think about hitchhikers, maybe the visions weren't so silly.

4

"Good-bye," she said positively. His hand tightened on her arm, and he smiled, but his grip became quite firm and hard. He was a very unpleasant young man, she decided, big shoulders and muscles and all, and she had had enough of him. She turned away decisively to walk into the café, discovering to her horror that his grip was immovable. She had half collided with a man coming out of the café, a smallish man in faded dungarees who smiled apologetically while Helen was starting to apologize.

"Is there something wrong?" the little man asked, and the beautiful young man glared at him.

"The young lady and I are having a conversation," he said in French.

"We are not having a conversation," Helen corrected him in French. "The young man wishes to travel in my car, and I have told him no. I don't know the young man." (How do you say "I don't know him from Adam" in French? "I cannot distinguish him from Adam"? Probably something idiomatic and quite different.) She jerked her arm to free it from his grasp.

The man in dungarees looked calmly at the beautiful young man and said, "Well?"

"This is none of your business," Berry snarled. "On your way!"

An excessively unpleasant young man, even when he spoke French. The man in dungarees didn't go away. He smiled in amusement and looked the young man up and down. Terribly insulting, Helen thought, and then thought, Good Lord, they may start fighting. She backed herself abruptly into the driving seat. The prospect of a street brawl as an introduction to France was unappealing. She pressed the starter and drove briskly away. In her side-view mirror she could see the handsome young man cursing at the man in dungarees and

5

turning as if to pursue her on foot. Mildly alarmed, she speeded up and traveled three blocks and then turned off to look for tea in some secluded side street. She was instantly cheered by the sight of another red Mini-Minor, the twin of her own car, parked outside a restaurant. There was an alley beside the restaurant, and she drove into this and parked, reflecting callously that if the place was crawling with hitch-hikers, they could accost somebody else next time. She was walking into the restaurant by the time Laurent, in the black Citroën, nosed round the corner of the street.

The sight of the zinc-topped tables cheered her at once, and so did the obscure fragrance of chocolate and wine and tobacco. Even the tea, which she had feared might be a novel experience, tasted quite like tea in spite of a haunting trace of some chemical. Probably chlorine in the water. The little restaurant was agreeably dark after the glare of the streets, and she surrendered herself to enjoyment of her situation. It was a pity, in a way, that she was on her way to spend the holiday with her sister—left to herself, she would rather have been entirely alone.

Still, it was generous of Rosemary to have insisted, and France was still France, even with relatives present. She closed her eyes gratefully and warned herself not to nod off at the table. Maybe it hadn't been very wise to drive all the way in one go. She was angry with herself when she realized that she must have nodded momentarily. A yell had jolted her back to the world. She looked up in bewilderment to see a tubby man in a linen jacket hurtling out of the restaurant.

"It's gone!" he howled from the pavement. The few customers were crowding to the door, and a middle-aged Englishwoman was preparing to have rollicking hysterics. Still shaken, Helen went to the door, where the tubby man seized on her.

"It was right here," he sobbed. "It's got . . . everything's in it! The lot! Did you see it?"

"What's happened?" Helen asked helplessly. The tubby man was thunderstruck.

"My ruddy car's been pinched, that's what's happened. Didn't you see it?" She shook her head.

"You must have seen it!" He shouted. "It's got everything in it; we only arrived this morning! A fifty-quid camera!"

His wife had appeared on the pavement, still unsure whether to have her hysterics or to wait till later. The tubby man raced along the street, and he suddenly turned round.

"Hey, it's here all the time!" He was looking into the alley-way, and Helen started to say, "No, that's my car," but he had already seen the number plate and was outraged afresh.

"It's exactly the same as mine!" he accused her, hating her because her car hadn't been stolen. "It's the last ruddy time I go abroad. You can't trust any of them."

"I'm very sorry my car hasn't been stolen," she said dryly. "Cars are stolen in England, too." Unconsciously she used the same tone in which she warned her schoolchildren not to generalize from the particular.

"Who the hell asked you to stick your nose in?" the tubby man demanded. "*You're* all right."

It was really absurd. She forced herself not to be angry with him by reminding herself that if anybody had stolen her darling little car, she would have died of fury. But he looked almost ready to strike her in his hurt and rage, except that he had now turned to his wife and was yelling at her that she must have seen who did it.

Helen shrugged and went in to pay her bill. Somebody inside the café was saying that the police must be called. Everybody shouted at once, and there was a fine holiday air of ex-

7

citement. The tubby man came in breathing fire, and she made a last effort at friendliness.

"Would you like me to telephone the police for you?" she offered.

"I don't need any advice from you!" he snarled. She shrugged again and went out. It seemed craven to desert a fellow countryman in trouble, but there are limits. It also seemed nice not to be mixed up in any police nonsense. In spite of her determined fair-mindedness, Helen found she had a parochial distrust of foreign policemen.

At least she wasn't having a dull holiday. She smiled to herself, backed out of the alleyway and carefully drove away. The sun really was very bright, it blazed on the dusty street and forced her to screw up her eyes. For the first time since leaving home, she began to think that perhaps a short nap was even more desirable than driving nonstop to China. Why not? She could get into open country, find a beach and sleep for an hour . . . a nice beach with families picnicking on it, not a deserted beach concealing hitchhikers or car thieves. She screwed her eyes a little tighter and drove with infinite care.

As a result, she had time to see something familiar in a figure walking ahead of her. As she drew abreast, she slowed down and became sure that it was the same man, the man in dungarees who had rescued her from the importunate hitchhiker. She stopped and called out to him.

"Yes, mademoiselle?" It was positively the same man. He was carrying a bag of tools.

"Can I give you a lift?" The words came out unthinkingly, for want of anything else to say. He waggled a hand in refusal.

"Ah, it's not necessary, mademoiselle." (How does he

8

know I'm a mademoiselle?) "I am going to catch a car."

"Well, this is a car. Alors, c'est un car. . . ." (No, of course, "car" is a bus in French.) "I mean, you are welcome."

"I am going to Saint-Tombe, mademoiselle." His shrug indicated that she couldn't possibly be going so far.

"So am I," she said, and smiled. "What an agreeable coincidence."

"Ah."

"Well?" she said.

"Ah. One must be very careful, mademoiselle. You don't know me." He smiled, and Helen smiled in return. He shrugged his shoulders and walked round the car to get in.

"You are very kind, mademoiselle."

"Not at all." She was aware of the irony of refusing a lift to a stranger and deliberately offering a lift to another.

"Turn right, mademoiselle."

"Thank you." She changed gear carefully. "Do you live in Saint-Tombe?"

"Yes."

He sat with his bag on his lap and his hands resting on it, silent and relaxed. She found herself self-conscious, nervous of changing gear clumsily. Open country stretched before her.

"I must thank you," she said, staring straight ahead.

"Nothing, nothing."

"You know this countryside well?"

"Well enough, I use the road often." He still sat quite still, and then said, "Would you like me to describe the countryside? Some people prefer to be silent while driving."

"Yes, I'm rather tired," she admitted. "The sun is very bright."

"Would you like me to drive for you, mademoiselle?"

9

"No, no." The idea of turning her cherished little car, the beloved act of driving, over to somebody else was unthinkable. Then she realized it was even more absurd to think it unthinkable. Her eyes began to ache from the glare. She traveled a mile before she decided she could find the right tone of voice in which to change her mind casually.

"Perhaps, after all," she said. "I am very tired."

"Of course." He opened the door as she stopped, and got out. "I shall drive with great care, mademoiselle. I am a garagiste."

"Good."

She watched his sinewy hands on the wheel furtively, looked at the road ahead and found her eyes insisted on closing. She giggled, but the man in dungarees didn't look round. He was equally relaxed at the wheel and driving, she realized, at a steady seventy. He seemed extremely competent. She was giggling at the thought that she was going to fall asleep and that it was an ideal situation for rape, murder, robbery, anything. She tilted her seat back and stretched her legs and allowed her eyes to close.

The garagiste looked round at her and took the opportunity of studying her face closely. Then he turned back to the road and drove on, whistling without sound. Helen's head had nodded forward on her chest.

On a quiet little beach just out of sight of the road as Helen was sped unconscious toward Saint-Tombe, Laurent was leaning against the fender of the black Citroën and sneering at Berry. Berry was combing through a heap of luggage in the back of a red Mini-Minor and cursing.

"It's your fault," he told Laurent. "You said this was the car." Laurent said nothing. Berry straightened up.

10

"This is something, at least." He brandished a 35 mm. camera in a polished new leather case.

"Put it back," Laurent told him. Berry glared at Laurent; Laurent continued to stare coldly at Berry.

"You would like to be caught with a stolen camera worth two hundred francs? Okay, keep the car and the camera, I'll go on alone."

Berry cursed again, threw the camera on the ground and kicked it. Laurent opened the passenger door of the Citroën, gave a mocking bow and said, "May I drive monsieur somewhere?"

"Very funny," said Berry.

2 ON THE SMALLER BEACH AT SAINT-TOMBE,

Helen's sister Rosemary and her husband Albert Moore were comfortable in deck chairs. Between them was a folding picnic table. The beach was hardly more than a triangular cove of steep sand, enclosed by a miniature cliff of black rock. Their two children Roddy and Vanessa were playing near the water, and Rosemary scanned the beach from time to time to identify them among the other children.

"Lovely sunshine," she said.

"Yup, it's the life, all right," said Albert.

Rosemary limply fingered a slightly out-of-date *Daily Express*.

"There's a heat wave in England," she said.

"Oh? That's a change."

Rosemary felt vaguely aggrieved by the idea of a heat wave in England. It wasn't fair that people who stayed at home should have sunshine when she had spent money to travel to France for sunshine. It spoiled the pleasure of going home with a sun tan. She comforted herself with the probability that the English heat wave would end in thunderstorms, possibly followed by snow. She helped herself to another chocolate. Albert poured himself a glass of white wine from a thermos flask and switched on the portable radio. He looked at his watch. Albert wasn't worried about the heat wave in England. He felt fine. He was a bulky man of forty who had been well built ten years ago and was now fat. His hair was black and dense, and he wore a thin, rather raffish mustache.

"Helen should be here soon," he muttered.

"She won't arrive for hours," Rosemary said. "You know Helen, old twenty-miles-an-hour. She's probably lost somewhere, she's got no experience of traveling."

Albert showed slight alarm.

"I should have driven over to meet her," he said; and his wife returned, a little inconsistently, "She's perfectly capable of finding her own way on a straight road."

"I hope so," said Albert, and shifted uneasily in his deck chair. Rosemary shot him a glance that was not so much suspicion as full knowledge of his mental processes. Men got the same ideas about any woman, even their own sisters-in-law; not that Helen was any young glamour girl, but Albert would look sideways at *anything* in skirts. He had to be treated like a child in some ways. She thought peevishly about the English heat wave again and shouted to Vanessa not to get her hair wet.

"You'd better go down there," she told Albert. "She never pays any attention to me."

"Ah, hell, let her hair get wet," Albert muttered. "What'll we do tonight? We could show Helen the night life."

"*We* will go out," Rosemary said menacingly. "Helen's not going to be in any mood for night life after her journey. Anyway, somebody has to watch the kids."

"God, is that why you invited her?" Albert demanded. "As a baby sitter on the cheap? We've got Marie."

13

"I don't trust Marie, and I don't want to hear any more about it."

"My God, you're cool!" Albert said, and then abandoned the subject and found another station on the radio. Rosemary nodded to herself and picked up the most expensive of her French magazines and took another chocolate. The captions in the magazine irritated her slightly because they weren't given in English, but the pictures were expensive and the dresses were expensive and there was a nice expensive feeling about the paper. Unconsciously she glanced round to make sure the car was still standing on the road above the beach. It was a Cresta in three tones with a green plastic sun visor and imitation leopard upholstery. Like Helen, Rosemary loved her car, though to her sorrow she hated motoring. To look at it was enough. It was expensive and it looked expensive. Her clothes were expensive too, the radio was expensive and everything was of the best. Rosemary had what she wanted. The only things that bothered her were the English heat wave, Albert's sullenness at not being allowed to show Helen the town, and the fact that Vanessa was now playing at the other end of the beach, several yards away from the water, instead of getting properly wet and enjoying herself when she had the expensive opportunity. Vanessa was an irritating child.

She found consolation in anticipating her sister's arrival. Albert would sniff round Helen, pulling his stomach in and trying to look athletic and patting her bottom every chance he got, the way he did with every woman, but there was nothing really serious in that. He would *not* take Helen out to see the town. Helen wasn't the kind for sophisticated pleasures; she was a settled old spinster even if she was only four years older than Rosemary, and she liked housework and she liked kids. Spinsters always liked kids, mostly because they weren't stuck with them all day long. Helen would be more reliable with Roddy and Vanessa than Marie, the French girl who came in to help in the kitchen, and it would be a rest and a nice change for Helen to have plenty of quiet evenings in the house, after the strain of the funeral and everything.

Rosemary had everything sorted out, and she knew from experience that everything would work out her way because it was only reasonable. She enjoyed the knowledge of her generosity in inviting her sister to share the family holiday as soon as father died. Helen had made out she didn't want to come, didn't want to be a nuisance, but it stood to reason she needed her own relations round her. After living with father for all those years, she would be lost on her own.

Rosemary even reflected that she could let Helen have two or three of her own dresses—not old, none of her dresses was old. Chic dresses, the kind Helen couldn't buy for herself. Rosemary smiled in satisfaction at the thought and narrowed her eyes to run over the possibles. The snag was she couldn't actually spare any of the dresses she had with her. Still, she could *tell* Helen she had two or three nice ones at home to give her. Two, anyway.

"Mm, it's getting late." Albert sat up with the surprised expression he always used when he wanted to seem casual. He glowered at his watch. "I tell you what—I could take a run up to the house to check if Helen's arrived and then come back down for you."

"You'll do nothing of the kind," Rosemary told him. "Go down and get the kids and we'll all go up. This sun's too hot anyway, it's beginning to give me a headache."

At the sound of the old warning word "headache" Albert couldn't resist a sly suggestion.

"You won't feel like going out tonight, then, with a headache. . . . Hey Roddy!" he shouted, before she could answer. "Come on, get Vanessa and come up, your mother wants you!"

On this occasion they were able to assemble the children and get them loaded into the car without any mutinies, with the promise that Aunt Helen was on her way. As they approached the little house in a back street above the town, Albert gave a muttered damn. A little red car was already standing in the street in front of the house.

"Well, she's arrived," Rosemary retorted. "There's nothing to swear about."

There was a wrought-iron bench inside the tiny courtyard, and Helen was sitting on it, reading a book, looking quite unworried and composed; looking like a competent spinster aunt, perhaps. She rose to greet them so amiably that Rosemary was stricken with shame at not having been home to welcome her and slightly nettled that Helen didn't appear to mind.

Helen did mind, but after twelve years of keeping house for a widowed father, and several years of teaching school infants, she had acquired a firm habit of discarding feelings that consumed energy without making any profit. She embraced Rosemary and submitted to a bear hug from Albert that was more or less brotherly. It was nice, after all, to have people of one's own at the end of a journey. The children had grown beyond all recognition since the last time she had seen them. Roddy at ten was shaping up to be a true son of Albert, with heavy shoulders and limbs and a bullet head of wiry black hair. At seven, Vanessa was leggy and pale, and her eyes were dark and shadowed. Constipation, Helen thought, with a slight pursing of the lips. Too many sweets and not enough roughage. Suddenly she heard herself thinking and laughed at the sound. Vanessa laughed back at her, eager, nervous, anxious to join in.

"Did you bring us anything?" Roddy demanded, and Albert laughed in approval.

"He knows how to get on with women already!"

"Yes," Helen told Roddy coolly. "You may even get it, if you behave yourself. After I wash."

"Oh-oh. No bath," Rosemary said. Helen wrinkled her nose and then shrugged.

"As long as there's water."

"Do like the French, Helen," Albert advised her. "Bags of Eau de Cologne and skip the water!" Helen smiled her appreciation of his wit. Vanessa, who had said nothing, was staring at her with a fixed, eager expression; like a dog waiting to be taken out? No, like a child who knows that life is wonderful and is waiting for it to start happening. Helen reached out and ruffled Vanessa's stringy hair, and the little girl grinned and flushed deep scarlet. For a moment, after all those years, Helen envied Rosemary.

"Come on, I'll get your presents first," she said.

"You don't look dirty anyway," said Roddy. Rosemary tutted in conventional disapproval of spoiling the brats, and Helen rummaged in the back of the car to find the presents. Vanessa got a giant inflatable beach ball, and Roddy a compass on a wrist strap. In a second, Vanessa was jumping up and down in a transport of joy, blowing the thing up in inadequate little gasps. Roddy glared at the compass.

"It's got no winder," he complained.

"It's not a watch, dummy, it's a compass. Look—the needle points to the north. You can tell any direction if you turn your hand round."

"It's only got one hand," he muttered. He sounded, Helen

17

feared, like a fairly stupid little boy. Vanessa, with her ball half inflated, was shouting, "Come and play with my ball, Roddy!"

Roddy glowered at her and said, "It's not your ball, it's *our* ball."

"It's mine!" Vanessa screamed.

"Selfish selfish," Rosemary chid her. "I don't know where she gets it from. Everything's Mine Mine Mine."

"I'll burst it," Roddy warned his sister, and Helen told him, "If you burst it, Roddy, I'll burst you." He eyed her, calculating her strength, and was rewarded with a practiced schoolmarm stare. "They always go and burst," he muttered.

It was foolish of her, Helen reflected, to have expected that Rosemary's children would be little angels. Five years of teaching should have taught her that no children are little angels. Still, even nonangelic children could grow on you. Young Roddy was now gazing resentfully at the compass on his wrist, and his thought processes were clearly visible through his black-haired skull: He would rather have had a watch, and he was going to bide his time and burst Vanessa's beach ball. Helen braced herself, not without pleasure, to the prospect of a fortnight in which she would improve the characters of the two children. That's what spinster aunts were for. She went indoors to wash all over from a basin of tepid water in her bedroom, and on an impulse, slapped on bags of Eau de Cologne. It felt wonderfully cool and sharp. She put on a clinically plain, straight dress of navy cotton, and was rewarded by Albert's eyebrows rising in open lechery when she came down to the courtyard. Well, well, she thought.

But all he said was, "How's the car? Get it through Customs all right?"

"They didn't even open it," she said. "The trouble is on the way home, surely, isn't it?"

"Oh, you can never tell with these French Customs," Rosemary assured her, from her superior experience, and started to describe an encounter with a particularly obnoxious French official. A delicate mechanism in Helen's brain advised her that there was going to be a lot of this during the next fortnight. Rosemary had had four Continental holidays while Helen had never been out of Scotland until this moment, and Rosemary would therefore have to guide and instruct Helen on every aspect of the mysterious Abroad in order to prevent Helen from getting above herself. Even Helen's ownership of a car all her own was a matter of concern and apprehension to Rosemary. At that moment Albert was outside unloading it and checking that the wheels hadn't fallen off through careless female driving.

"You've got to watch driving in France," said Rosemary, who had never driven in her life. "These French drivers are maniacs, some of them."

"Yes," Helen said slyly. "One of them drove me all the way here." Rosemary stared at her, stupefied, and Helen described how she had given a lift to a Frenchman and then handed over the wheel to him. Rosemary's horror was so catastrophic that Helen decided she had better not relate her other amusing French experience of being accosted by *another* Frenchman.

"Did you hear that?" Rosemary squeaked to Albert. "She gives a lift to a perfect stranger—a foreigner—and then lets him drive the car while she falls asleep, if you please!"

Rosemary's dramatic horror was in character, but Helen was exasperated when Albert too joined in the chorus. His jaw quite positively dropped.

"What did he look like?" he demanded. "Who was he? You

must be—my God, Helen, you must be stark bonkers!"

"He was a nice little Frenchman, his name is Paul Pennard, and he's a respectable tradesman of this village." Her lips pursed, a habit she had noticed of late and which distressed her. "You talk as if every foreigner was an escaped lunatic."

Albert had laid down a suitcase and he was breathing heavily.

"Now don't come the innocent, Helen," he said angrily. "You don't pick up strange men in this country. . . . How do you . . . He could have been . . ."

"What are *you* getting so worked up about?" Rosemary asked him, annoyed at Albert crowding into the act.

"Well, I'm here!" Helen tried not to lose her temper. Several further remarks came into her mind—I'm a grown woman . . . I can take care of myself . . . I'm not a child. . . . Odd how every reasonable retort to this hysteria sounded childish and pathetic. She bottled her anger and said nothing. Albert, striving for speech and finding none either, stamped back out to the car, and Rosemary, anxious to be friends, finished a little plaintively.

"We're only thinking of you, Helen—you don't *know* anything about foreign countries."

"O.K." Helen accepted the overture, and the temperature returned to normal. When Albert came back in he had evidently considered the matter and decided it was all right, this once.

"You shouldn't give us heart attacks, Helen," he said with a heavy attempt at affection. "Anyway, you're here, jolly bong." He sat down beside her and patted her knee, a second or two longer than was necessary. His hand had black strong hairs growing on the backs of the fingers. In spite of his childishness and his spurious brotherly love, Helen decided she quite liked him and that she was rather glad she wasn't married to him. Rosemary noticed his hand on Helen's knee but ignored it. She hoped the hard feelings had entirely vanished so that the atmosphere would be propitious for friendly talk about how Helen would enjoy staying home and keeping an eye on the kids for the evening.

Helen, sensitive as a cat, could hear Rosemary's mind working. She was already resigned to a quiet evening in the house by the time Rosemary slowly, slowly, started to explain how much she would enjoy a quiet evening in the house.

What was the point of struggling? There was still a fortnight ahead, and Rosemary couldn't ask her to stay at home every single evening.

"I've just had an idea," Albert said, in the middle of all this. "We can all have a nip in the pub next door before Rosemary and I go downtown. Eh?"

Rosemary's first reaction was hostility, but having settled the main problem to her satisfaction, she decided to be magnanimous. The little pub was so close that they could hear if one of the children yelled. As the idea grew on her, she began to explain enthusiastically to Helen that this quaint pub was a discovery of hers—absolutely French, with old stone-topped tables . . . slummy, but spotlessly clean, of course. A lovely change from those tourist traps. The children were forced under protest to bed, Roddy promising that he would have a nightmare within five minutes, and Helen and Albert and Rosemary walked round to the little pub.

Rosemary kept up a running commentary on the quaintness and Frenchness of it so that Helen wouldn't be stunned with shock on seeing it. It turned out to be a notably ordinary little place with a small bar counter at one end and three tables along one side. The staff was the tall, thin owner and his short, fat wife. The customers were four French-looking artisans, to whom Albert shouted a jovial bong soir. One of them was the garagiste to whom Helen had given a lift.

He half rose and raised a hand in greeting.

"Just ignore it," Rosemary muttered.

"It's Monsieur Pennard," Helen said. "My chauffeur." Rosemary tightened her lips.

"Is that a fact?" Albert looked at Pennard and threw away all his suspicions of strange Frenchmen. "Come and have a drink, monsieur," he shouted. "No, I insist. Une chaise."

Pennard came over and bowed faintly to Helen and Rosemary. Albert pushed a chair round for him.

"Cognac?" he said. "Well! Monsieur Pennard. You—live—Saint—Tombe?" He pronounced the words slowly, as to a deaf mute on the telephone.

"Yes," said Pennard. He was not quite so small as Helen had remembered—only smallish for a man. And not so old. She had only just recognized him, possibly because he was wearing a dark jacket and a white shirt instead of dungarees. It was the thin, leathery look that made him seem smaller and middle-aged.

"Oh? You speak English?" Rosemary was taken aback. Pennard tilted his head.

"A few words, madame." Helen looked at him with fresh interest and thought, you sly dog, you.

"Vous ne m'avez pas dit ça, monsieur," she scolded him.

"Ah, il n'y avait pas de besoin, mademoiselle."

Rosemary shook her head wearily.

"It's no use trying to talk to them in French," she said. "They don't speak the same French in France as you learned in school." Pennard looked from Rosemary's mouth to Helen's face, questioning.

"Ma sœur me dit," Helen explained, "que votre français et mon français, monsieur, ce sont des languages tout à fait différents." He nodded wisely.

"Ah, les sœurs," he said, and Helen thought, Hm, what a shrewd little Frenchman.

"You stick in, Helen," Albert encouraged her. "You'll pick it up, you know. Practice." He drank, and they all drank. Suddenly, Helen felt embarrassed for her garagiste. She didn't want him to be displayed for the inspection of Rosemary and Albert. She finished her drink and declared that she must go back to the house, and Rosemary agreed that one cognac was quite enough when you didn't have a head for it. They all stood up, and Pennard shook hands with them. And suddenly Helen was more embarrassed for Albert and Rosemary than for him. He was a most self-contained man, utterly at ease. She had a swift flare of resentment when Rosemary, outside the pub, said grudgingly, "He seems all right." Helen decided not to answer.

"We won't be late," Albert assured her, as they left her in what was now the inky blackness of the night. "Just leave your car in the street, it's O.K. there."

She went back into the house and checked on the children, who miraculously were asleep. She would sit and read a book and enjoy being quiet and savoring the feeling of being in France at last.

But she found herself restless. The furniture in the cramped little tall, thin French house was sound and adequate, but it didn't include a comfortable armchair—evidently chairs in France were for sitting on during a meal and nothing else. She decided to go up and read in bed.

Once there, she had no urge to read. She opened the little window wide and leaned out, feeling like a romantic adolescent. The night was intensely dark except where the

23

light from the pub nearby picked up the pale blur of a mimosa bush. Mimosa! Real mimosa growing wild. She hugged herself. Then she decided that in spite of Albert's assurance, she would feel better with her beloved little car tucked safely inside the courtyard. She slipped downstairs and dragged open the iron gate and drove through with infinite care, with headlamps full on. When she switched them off she was quite dizzy with the jolt of darkness. She wandered round the courtyard trying to savor the Frenchness of it as she stumbled and shook herself into rationality and went back upstairs.

French houses, she discovered, also regarded electric light as something to be used briefly to prevent accidents and then switched off. It was not for squandering on reading in bed. The solitary lamp in her room was a dingy little bare bulb of around fifteen watts dangling from the geometric center of the ceiling. She tried grimly to read crouched forward in bed, but the type swam in the half-light, and she finally decided that fate meant her to get to sleep like a good girl. She padded across the tiled floor and switched the lamp off.

It was difficult to sleep, but in Helen's life it was often difficult to sleep. She refrained, by long habit and training, from tossing and turning. She arranged her body comfortably and lay perfectly still, and eventually she began to be aware of the small twists of illogic in her thoughts that preceded sleep. Then she was awake.

It was still as black as outer space. It was uncomfortably warm. There must have been a noise. She strained her ears in the darkness for a sound from the children. A faint movement, but it seemed to come from the direction of the window. Probably Albert and Rosemary coming home, and therefore it was foolish to get up and stare out, but she was up and staring out, and the courtyard below was still like a hole into hell. Nevertheless, something was moving, something was making faint noises.

"Is that you, Albert?" she called. The silence was now quite noticeable, a sudden cessation of sound. Helen gazed quite calmly down into the darkness, controlling the nervous quickening of her breath. It was probably a cat (she remembered irrelevantly that she hadn't seen a single cat in the streets since she had arrived in France). A dog? If it was a cat or a dog, it was nothing to worry about.

If it was a prowling human being, she was safe nevertheless. She was upstairs; the downstairs door was locked. (Was it? Yes, it was.) There was a pub nearby, houses, people. If anyone tried to come into the house, she could switch lights on and scream.

The silence continued. She grew angry, both at whatever had caused the noise and at herself. Some idiot teen-ager, perhaps, hoping to steal something from her car. There was nothing worth stealing in the car. But inane children sometimes wrenched off side-view mirror, license plates, scratched the paintwork just for kicks. The idea infuriated her. She found the light switch and turned it, put on slippers and a dressing gown, and ran downstairs. Half sure that there was nothing in the courtyard at all, she had no intention of taking any risks. She switched on the light in the kitchen, to let it spill into the courtyard, and went to the window and looked out. The light fell on the little car, but there was no sign of human or animal. She went to the kitchen door and opened it, but kept her hand on the knob ready to slam it shut. The silence was complete.

It was clear that she had imagined the sound. She was

25

unhysterical enough to know that everybody can become hysterical occasionally. It was hysterical, for instance, to want to slam the door to and bolt it when the courtyard was empty. She forced herself to step beyond the threshold and look all round the yard.

Something soft and black covered her head. Her hands came up to ward it off and she screamed. But her scream went into the dark material, and it pressed against her face. Now, she thought briefly, I am hysterical. If I go limp, I'll be safe. But she didn't go limp. She strove to free her arms and throw off the covering from her face. Mad with fear she saw herself dead and struggled with staring eyes to breathe as the cloth pressed irresistibly into her mouth, her nostrils. She was drowning in darkness, dead after all, dead, dead. She went limp, too late.

3 $\approx\approx\approx\approx\approx\approx\approx$ *WHEN HELEN CAME ROUND, THE FIRST THING* she registered was that Albert was drunk and Rosemary was angry. She was sitting awkwardly in one of the kitchen chairs, and Albert's face was very close and shiny. He was holding a glass of brandy inaccurately to her mouth. She shook her head to escape from the glass.

"Somebody threw something over my head," she said dully. She was shivering. Rosemary stared at her, Albert stared at her. Albert's eyes were very slightly crossed, which made his grave expression look imbecilic.

"What do you mean?" Rosemary asked, and turned to Albert as if Helen weren't there. "She's still dopey. We'd better get her to bed. This is great, I don't think. What's got into you, Helen?" Helen regarded her numbly and went on shivering.

"Somebody threw something over my head," she insisted. Albert stood up, waggling his head to clear it. Rosemary, with a swift gesture, put her arms round Helen and fondled her hair.

"You're all right now, darling, we're here. There, there. Maybe there *was* somebody outside," she added to Albert.

"Nobody there now," he said thickly.

27

"What do you expect?" Rosemary asked testily. "Come on, dear, we'll get you to bed."

"Call the police," Helen said. Her voice felt stupid, drunk, and she drew a shuddering gasp of breath.

"I dunno where the police 'ation is," Albert complained. "Never even seen a policeman. Who was it?"

"I couldn't see anything!" Helen wailed.

"We'll call the police first thing in the morning," Rosemary assured her. "There aren't any marks on your face, Helen—no bruises or anything." Helen pulled her dressing gown shut, and Rosemary protested, "I was only looking to see if there were any bruises."

Helen stood up.

"Somebody threw something over my head—" She clenched her teeth and her fists to stop the shivering. "We'll talk about it in the morning," she said.

"Sa good idea," Albert agreed, and added thoughtfully, drunkenly, "Don' want the police when the car's outside an' I've been on the booze. Sleep on it, that's the idea. I'll juss take a look." He wheeled round and cannoned out of the kitchen into the courtyard. "Nobody here now," he shouted. Helen leaned on the table and found it was easier to stop shivering by letting her body go loose than by clenching. She breathed in deep sobs.

"That's probably wakened the kids," Rosemary muttered and flew upstairs. Albert shambled back into the kitchen.

"Tell you what, we'll leave the outside light lit. Light lit. Thar'll keep them away. Was it that Frenchman?" he asked, on a sudden inspiration. Helen shook her head, knowing the impossibility of explaining anything.

"Thank heavens the kids are still sound," Rosemary said. "Now come on, you'd better lie down, Helen."

28

Helen carefully picked up the glass of brandy from the table and drained it.

"Try and get some sleep," she said, with an edge of hysteria, and when Rosemary nodded, she explained, "That's what they always say in the pictures when somebody's had his leg clawed off by a tiger. Try and get some sleep." She tried to stop grinning, sure that she looked hideous. Rosemary put an arm round her and helped her upstairs.

"Are you sure you're all right?"

"Yes, bronzed and fit." Her teeth chattered on the words as she pulled the blankets round her.

"Try and get—you'll feel better in the morning," Rosemary said. "You're all right now."

It was rough on Rosemary, Helen knew. Illnesses or crises exhausted Rosemary; they made life awkward for everybody. Helen lay flat on her back and stared at the blackness of the ceiling. If she concentrated on relaxing, the shivering stopped.

We are the prisoners of our nervous systems, she thought. Nothing is changed, I am lying safely in bed, I'm healthy and unharmed, I'm fit and sane and warm. I can't stop shivering, damn it. Damn the central nervous system and the adrenalin glands. I'm going to have a wonderful holiday. In the morning I'll say that and believe it. Why can't I believe it now? Damn endocrinology.

A small spot of warmth made itself felt in her chest and gradually spread. Three cheers for alcohol.

Through the timber wall on her right she could hear Albert and Rosemary moving about and murmuring to each other.

"It's the heat and all that drink, she's not used to it," Rosemary said. The wall was not so much a barrier as a sounding board. That was going to be wildly entertaining for the next fortnight, Helen thought, shuddering as she changed position in bed.

"You were worried enough downstairs." Albert.

"You can never tell, with these foreigners." Rosemary.

Shuffle and creak.

"I don't like it." Albert. "Don' want people snooping about."

"Did you leave the outside light on?"

"Sure thing. Electricity's included in the rent."

"Gas as well?"

"No, we pay f' gas sepr'ly."

"Oh."

"I don' like it."

"Well, stop staring out of the window and come to bed."

" 'F there's anybody snooping round I'll kill them."

"Albert, do you think Helen's developing funny ideas—about that car?"

"Wha' the hell are you talking about?"

"You wouldn't know, you never read anything. You know, spinsters, at that age, dogs and cats—they get funny about things. There's a name for it."

"Fetichism," Helen whispered to herself. "Fetichism's the name."

"I think you're talkin' a load of old rubbish." Albert.

"You don't know everything." Rosemary. "Come away from that window, you'll get a chill. That's all I need, two of you to nurse. Some holiday."

"O.K., O.K."

Shuffle shuffle shuffle creak.

"Aren't you going to put the light out?" Rosemary.

"Hell."

Creak shuffle shuffle shuffle. Click. Shuffle shuffle.

"Damn an' blast!"

Creak.

"Well, spinsters do get funny."

"Ah, belt up for God's sake."

"Turn round the other way."

"F'God's sake, I wasn't trying anything."

"I didn't say you were."

"Waaa."

Creak.

Helen was sure that if she giggled, the giggle would be hysterical, a nervous reaction. She bit the edge of a blanket.

It will all look different in the morning. Maybe in the morning I'll decide I simply had a fainting fit.

. . . Maybe I did simply have a fainting fit. . . .

No, it was a rational, an—an extraneous thing. Somebody threw something over me.

She shivered.

A dream is just as real as an extraneous thing.

Not in the same way.

Quite rational people can deceive themselves.

Like what, for instance? Like having a bag flung over their imaginary heads?

Spinsters—God, stop thinking and get to sleep—spinsters are prone to imagination . . . untapped nervous energy. Like spinsters who keep seeing men pursuing them, accosting them.

I'm not that kind of spinster.

A man accosted you at Le Touquet.

Well, he *did* accost me—he only wanted a lift. That's an objective fact.

You accosted a *man.*

Ah, for God's sake belt up, will you? You're talkin' a load of old rubbish.

She slept sporadically, without enjoying it.

Berry and Laurent sat in the big Citroën in the darkness. They were not enjoying each other's company.

"I say we should go back and finish the job," said Berry.

"You mean kill her properly?" Laurent was tired of Berry.

"That one isn't old enough to kill," Berry said, with a leer in his voice. "She feels all right in the dark, huh?"

Laurent refused to rise this time. "The big man wouldn't feel so nice. He's a strong one, that one."

"Fft!" Laurent made a noise to indicate derision and a knife across a throat simultaneously.

"Brave little boy," Laurent said, without much interest. Berry was suddenly vicious and frustrated.

"We'll miss our chance altogether!" he swore. "We haven't got time to waste."

"We have time," said Laurent. "Not with lights shining and people waiting for us to come back at night. We tried, we failed. Listen, junior, we can't afford any trouble on this job. Quietly, when nobody's looking, get that into your head. A smashed car is one thing, a corpse is another."

"I don't see the difference."

"The difference is nobody is going to get worried about a smashed car, we get plenty of time to get away. We need time after the job's done."

Laurent spoke coldly and rationally, as much to persuade himself as Berry. He had a half suspicion that Berry was right to be impatient, that he himself would botch the job through too much caution. That was why he had Berry with

32

him. He knew now he could never have come this far without Berry's greed and Berry's impatience to drive him on. Laurent had always been a careful man, but now he could almost believe he had completely lost his nerve. The prospect of danger unmanned him.

But for that, he wouldn't have needed Berry at all; the job was so simple. He disliked Berry, but he had talked himself into using him because he needed Berry's energy. Laurent had lost his old energy, and, though he concealed it from Berry, most of his nerve too. He had had the ironic misfortune to be busy blowing a safe in a Paris office when a patriotic citizen had thrown a plastic bomb into the office. The explosion had been an amateur botch, and Laurent was only mildly dazed. But it had shattered his professional faith in the predictability of chemical events. He couldn't even face the idea of retiring from his profession and going back to the coal mines.

The answer to his problems had come in one glorious flash of luck when his old coal mining mate Cabas had sought him out in Paris with news of a real prize—the legendary once-and-for-all jackpot, the life pension, the farewell to crime. And it didn't even require any safe blowing, guns or nasty business of any kind. All the nasty business had already been done very slickly by a high-class organization in which Cabas himself was a minor executive with private ambitions. He provided the information, Laurent was to do the work and the work was childishly simple—a matter of interrupting the delivery of the goods. All the same, Laurent had discovered that any work at all tended to paralyze his nerves. He needed support. He looked round his acquaintances, saw Berry having a thin time in an interval between mistresses, and took him into partnership.

33

Now that they were actually in Brittany, Laurent kept feeling that it would be nice if Berry would do something foolish and finish the job without him. If Berry could be trusted to finish the job, that is, and still remember Laurent's share in the partnership. There were also times when Laurent felt it might be pleasant to catch a cold, or have a painless broken leg, and retire from the job entirely. But what, afterward? The coal mines?

"We still have time," he told Berry. "In daylight, without trouble. If we can steal one car, we can steal another car."

"But where *is* it?" Berry asked. Berry was rubbing his fingers together, trying to use up the terrible energy of youth and greed. "We've got to know where it is."

"How many places can it be?" Laurent returned.

There had been a time when a good skinful would guarantee a sound sleep for Albert. Nowadays, he found, it produced quick coma for four hours, followed by a wakeful misery, gray and greasy. This time the misery was sharpened by sudden apprehension. He heaved himself out of bed and stumbled to the open window. Not a hangover, more like a residual drunkenness. The night, like his brain, was dark mottled gray, just light enough to mock the lamp burning outside the kitchen door. The little red car, curiously colored in the predawn light and smothered in dew, was standing lonely and forlorn. Albert breathed deeply and wrinkled his face at the sour taste. In his mind, he imitated a drunk man's speech.

Lesh juss lay off the booze slightly, Albert, ole boy. Juss for a coupla days. Then we can lerrit rip, ole boy ole boy.

He sighted the bedroom door with one eye closed and followed his pointing finger to the toilet.

4

4 *THE HEAT WAVE IN ENGLAND CONTINUED,* but cricket at Lord's had been stopped by a sudden thunderstorm. This was a consolation to Rosemary, reading a new but still out-of-date *Daily Express*.

"Except for the haze, I suppose you might see the Cornish cliffs from here," Helen said. They were sitting in the deck chairs at the small beach. Vanessa and Roddy were down at the water's edge, with the giant beach ball, and Roddy was contriving to punt it well into the sea regularly. The wind, Helen noticed, kept blowing it back to shore.

"Nah, they're hundreds of miles away," Albert told her. Having surrendered his deck chair to Helen, he was standing with hands in pockets, moodily kicking at the sand.

"Barely a hundred, surely," Helen protested, and Albert thought this over, wondering whether to stick to his story. Helen was often right about these things. It was one of the interesting things about Helen, but it was aggravating too. Albert understood women as well as men, and he knew how to handle both, but with the odd one like Helen, you got the feeling that they were thinking of something else all the time. You couldn't get to them. In any case, Albert had a more important problem.

"Do you want to go to the police?" he asked.

"What would you advise?" Helen dumped it right back in his lap, and you would swear she was doing it out of cussedness.

"You've just got to watch the consequences, that's all," he said. "So you start bothering the gendarmes—so what do they do? They bother you back. They've got nothing else to do in a dead hole like this. So they drop in every day for a chat, you've got them in your hair for the rest of the month. I'm just telling you what I think."

"Don't say anything about Helen, then," said Rosemary. "Say you saw a prowler last night, you don't need to go into details."

"What do you think, Helen?" Albert asked. Helen pulled up her skirt to let the sun fall on her thighs.

"I don't give a damn now," she said. Albert and Rosemary exchanged glances, and Rosemary nodded wisely. Albert came to a sudden decision, and Helen, with eyes closed, could sense that he had changed gear.

"I'll go and give them the patter," he offered. "Just to keep everybody happy. Hey, I'll take your car, Helen—then you can bring the family back in ours if I'm late." Helen began to think of a protest, but he was already picking up her keys from her open handbag and striding up the beach.

"Anybody would think your car was an only child," Rosemary chid her. "For heaven's sake, it was Albert that got it for you."

"Mm." It didn't matter. The sun struck through the fabric of her dress, soothing and delicious. The other families on the beach were all French, and the shouts in a long-loved language were music.

"That's Vanessa yelling again," Rosemary commented. "Moan moan moan—nothing ever pleases that child." Helen opened one eye and saw the big beach ball floating several yards from the shore; but it was still drifting in. She started to get up.

"I'll go and play with them," she offered.

"You'll get no thanks."

"I'll take them up on the rocks."

"Don't let them fall!"

Helen walked down the beach without bothering to answer. She was a bit too skinny, Rosemary told herself.

The children were all for climbing rocks. Helen deflated the beach ball and threw it up beside Rosemary, who took another chocolate and waved. The rocks looked high and forbidding, but they were easy to climb, with plenty of flat platforms and short jumps. Helen led the way till she realized that Vanessa was her superior as a climber and let the thin little girl scramble ahead. They rounded the cliff, out of sight of the beach, and kept climbing.

"Hey, I saw right up your skirt," Roddy yelled.

Helen stifled an urge to punch him.

"You'll know what color my bathing suit is, then," she said. No, she was exaggerating it. Roddy was merely behaving like a boy.

"Black!" he shouted in triumph. Vanessa was yelling from the top, jumping up and down and clapping her hands. Helen leaped up beside her, then sat on a patch of grass and looked out over the sea. It was glassy dark under the haze.

"Are you a historical spinster?" Roddy asked her. Vanessa yelled, "No, she's not! She's not!"

"I only *asked*," Roddy protested.

"I'm a spinster," Helen agreed.

"What is it?" Vanessa.

"I told you," Roddy sneered.

"You're a spinster too, Vanessa. It means you're not mar-ried yet."

"What's a historical spinster?"

"Queen Elizabeth," said Helen.

"Did Queen Elizabeth walk in her sleep?" Roddy per-sisted. Helen wasn't very worried that she should be described as a hysterical spinster, since she knew that she wasn't hys-terical. But it irked her that Rosemary had no more sense than to prattle her *Reader's Digest* psychology in front of the children. She felt sad and alone.

"Come on," she said, "I'll race you to the tree. Last is a sissy."

"I can beat you!" Roddy shouted.

"That'll be the day!" Helen told him. She flew across the rough grass with her hair streaming.

While Helen was asserting her youth and vigor, Albert was having an unpleasant shock. Having driven away from the beach in Helen's little car, he pondered carefully on the busi-ness of going to the police. If he didn't go, Helen or Rose-mary might ask him about it. He could say he had gone, but it was hard to fool two women. On the other hand, if he did go, there would be all the fuss of nosy policemen—foreign policemen—infesting the holiday and getting in the way.

He finally decided on the brilliant notion of having a quiet drink and then reporting that the local policeman hadn't been in. He didn't feel like talking to policemen. First he drove to the little house to pick up some fresh cigarettes. He didn't like French cigarettes, and was always careful to stock up on the boat coming over with English duty-frees. He parked outside the house and went into the courtyard to find a French policeman peering in at the kitchen window.

"What's up?" Albert was startled and guilty.

The policeman turned to him. The policeman was a thin, gloomy man with a dissatisfied face, and he took his time before speaking. He looked searchingly into Albert's face as if thinking of something else. The silence made Albert feel like a fool.

"Mr. Moore." It was a statement.

"Oui."

"You speak French, Mr. Moore?"

Albert waved his hand to dismiss such a foolish notion.

"Oui. Nong. Bong jour. That's my lot."

"Ah."

"Well, that knocks that on the head, dunnit?" Albert said cheerfully.

"I will try the English," the policeman said slowly after a pause.

"Suit yourself. What d'you want to know?" Albert spoke quickly. "Come inside, I need some fags."

The policeman followed him into the kitchen, and Albert carefully stood with his back to him while he opened a drawer and took out a twenty packet. There was no point in flashing several hundred Capstans in front of Nosy Parkers. The policeman stood without saying anything. One of these sad, silent sods.

"I don't suppose you want a drink."

"Please."

"Never seen a copper refuse one," Albert muttered. He poured two glasses of vermouth.

"Your good sister is attacked, Mr. Moore."

"Oh, that. Who told you that?"

"It is true?"

This was what came of Rosemary yakking to strangers in the café during the morning.

39

"She isn't my sister, she's my sister-in-law. Sister. In. Law. Get it? You're not very hot on the English, are you?" He felt like telling the thin, sad policeman to get to hell and mind his own business. He knew the type. The policeman was writing slowly in a small notebook.

"Sister-in-law," he said. Albert poured another shot of vermouth into the policeman's glass.

"Look, you don't want to bother with this, monsieur," he said. "It's all a storm in a teacup. Comprenny? A storm in a teacup." Albert made circular motions at his ear with one finger, and the policeman studied these with care. A numbskull, it stuck out a mile.

"At what hour she is attacked?"

"God knows. Look, have another drink, we're men of the world. You don't want to waste your time on this. Look, comprenny this. My sister-in-law—"

"Her name."

"Helen McLeish. Here, I'll write it down for you. She *thinks* she was attacked. O.K.? She is, what you say, imagination, comprenny? Beaucoup imagination, no?" The policeman stared at him with no expression at all.

"She is not attack," he said.

"You know what spinsters are." Well, it was true, Helen was a spinster, even if she wasn't *that* kind of spinster. The thing to do was to get rid of this mournful pest. "Look, monsieur, my sister-in-law, spinster, comprenny?"

"Spinster?"

"Not marry, eh? No husband . . . no . . . man." Albert found he was waving his flippers like a Frenchman—no wonder they flapped about so much, if everything was as hard to explain as this. He tapped his forehead. "Women get funny in head," he pointed out. "You know—woman, no man, no boy friend, beaucoup imagination, yes?"

"Ah." The policeman thoughtfully downed his vermouth. Albert refilled his glass.

"It's like this. She thinks she hears a noise, she gets out of bed, she faints. Faints, yes? Fall down? Thud? Sore head, too much cognac, no? She *think* somebody attack her."

"Vir-gin!"

"That's it, you're right on the ball, monsieur! Comprenny?" The word virgin sounded oddly obscene in a French accent, and it triggered off a series of small thumps in Albert's fantasy life, which was rudimentary and lacking in variety, but very pleasant to Albert.

"One will speak with Mademoiselle McLeish."

"Nong pas bother, monsieur. Forget all about it, that's your scheme."

"One will speak with Mademoiselle McLeish."

"Suit yourself, you'll get nowhere, I can tell you that."

Nothing could have dissuaded Jumeau from speaking with Mademoiselle McLeish. He was not very much interested in midnight attackers, and he had followed enough of Albert's conversation to gather that the sister-in-law was a virgin addicted to hallucinations. But life in the village of Saint-Tombe was a dull enough affair, and it was pleasant to talk to English tourists, with or without vermouth. Not many obscure police officers could speak English, and if one could, as Jumeau could, it was foolish not to keep in practice. Besides, he enjoyed the contact with the atmosphere of wealth, with the kind of tourists who always owned new cars and were careless with money.

"Well, I'm off," Albert said finally. He didn't intend to keep stoking this snooper up with free vermouth. A quiet noggin in a pub by himself without the wife and kids was the idea.

"I will come again, monsieur . . . Mister Moore," said Jumeau and followed him outside.

"Pretty little car," said Jumeau. "Very small."

"Yeah, it's all right. I run a big one myself."

"You have two cars?"

"No, this is my sister-in-law's."

In such families, even imaginative virgins had new cars. Jumeau leaned on the handlebars of his bicycle and pondered the strangeness of life. These people were not really wealthy, they considered themselves ordinary, but they took such things for granted. They would laugh if they knew that Jumeau was still hoping one day to be issued with a scooter. Albert started the Mini-Minor and roared down the hill. At that moment Marie, the French girl who helped Rosemary in the house, arrived to start preparing lunch. Jumeau watched her unlock the kitchen door and then followed her. She would know nothing, of course, but there was no harm in spending half an hour with her.

Marie knew nothing, but she helped Jumeau to another vermouth, and they passed the time agreeably talking about the strange habits of prosperous tourists and the cost of living while Marie peeled potatoes.

Rosemary was delighted with the way the holiday was working out. The excitement about the midnight prowler had been exasperating, but Helen seemed to have recovered and decided to be sensible. It would have been too frightful if she had really gone funny and become a nuisance, the way some women did. Instead, she had taken the kids away for over an hour and then brought them back and started teaching them French. . . . Roddy's first reaction was that talking

French was silly and sissy, but he soon became worried that Vanessa was getting one up on him, and he joined in doggedly to show that anybody could speak it. Rosemary sat and regarded this process indulgently. Anything would amuse kids, and it wouldn't do them any harm either—she could show them off to the neighbors back in Cricklewood, in fact. *That's the thing about traveling abroad, it gives the kids a great opportunity to learn the language naturally. . . .* She had got over her irritation at Helen's insistence on claiming to speak French. It stood to reason that when you didn't have a husband and kids to trot after all your life, you had time to waste on things like foreign languages—it was all you had, really, she told herself.

"Un deux trois," they chanted in the car while Helen maneuvered it up the hill from the beach. To Helen's surprise, it was not difficult after all to drive a big car. It was even easier than a small car, it moved so easily you hardly needed to change gear at all.

"Quatre cinq six," she chanted, and the two children bellowed it in response. They breasted the hill and started on the long high street to the house.

"Sept huit neuf!"

"Sept huit neuf!"

"I recognize that man," Helen said.

"Which man?" Rosemary looked round.

"He's gone."

"I hate meeting people from home," Rosemary remarked. "What's the use of going abroad and then meeting people from home?"

"No, it's a man I saw in Le Touquet—he asked me for a lift." Helen was puzzled. She didn't like it.

"*Another* one!" Rosemary refused to take her seriously.

43

"You'd better watch it, Helen, you'll be getting men on the brain."

"He asked me for a lift in Le Touquet," Helen insisted.

"But he's disappeared." Rosemary was off on her women's magazine psychology again.

"I was mistaken," Helen said thinly. "I didn't see him, and he never asked me for a lift either. It was two other people."

"I'm not saying that." Rosemary wasn't quite sure what she was saying. Helen breathed through her nose.

"Un deux trois," she chanted. Rosemary was happy to have the subject abandoned.

Jumeau had been careful not to have yet another vermouth, but the conversation had been so nice that he was still there when Helen and Rosemary arrived. He got slowly to his feet and resumed his grave official expression.

"Mademoiselle McLeish?"

"It's a French copper," Roddy told Vanessa.

"I know, I know!"

"C'est moi," Helen said. "Vous voulez discuter le . . . le . . . l'incident de hier soir?"

"It suffices to speak English, mademoiselle." Helen too found his fixed stare off-putting.

"Pas . . . pas avec les enfants . . . " she said. "Oh, all right, we can go outside."

"After you, mademoiselle."

"Hey, is he arresting you, Aunt Helen?" Roddy was clearly thrilled. Vanessa's lip trembled.

"He just wants to *talk* to Aunt Helen," Rosemary snapped. "Shut up, both of you."

Outside in the courtyard, Jumeau's manner was even slower than usual. The warmth of noon and the vermouth had worked on him. He gazed at the courtyard wall for several seconds.

"You suppose that one has attack you, mademoiselle."

"I suppose nothing of the kind, I'm not given to flights of fancy," Helen said crisply. Jumeau wrestled in stony silence with the rapid burst of English.

"Je ne suppose rien, monsieur," Helen said. "C'était une attaque véritable."

"It suffices to speak English, mademoiselle." Jumeau was offended by the suggestion that he couldn't understand English. "Why does it arrive, mademoiselle?" Helen looked blank, and they stared at each other. He repeated the question, more gravely.

"You mean *when*," she said. "Or *where*."

"I mean, mademoiselle, pray to speak the incident to me." It wasn't quite right, but perfectly clear. Mademoiselle was smiling to herself, and he found this offensive too. He could well believe that this one was imaginative. He couldn't quite admit to himself that he found her attractive—in a cold, sexless way, that is—and, like many attractive women, insultingly unimpressed by men. That little smile was intended as a sneer, or, possibly, it was an irrational smile. Such women imagined that all men were fascinated by them. He, Jumeau, was not so easily fascinated.

Helen, who very soon found herself smiling at Jumeau's ponderous, mildly drunken dignity and his ponderous, mildly drunken pidgin English, soon afterward realized that she had not found a friend in M. Jumeau. His principal object was to impress her with his command of English, and as far as his words had any meaning at all, they meant that he thought very little of her story that she had been attacked.

45

She wondered shrewdly if Albert had briefed him for the interview.

"I didn't ask you to come here, monsieur," she said, very precisely. "If you do not believe me, you may go."

"Ah."

"Good-bye."

"We will speak again, mademoiselle."

"Perhaps."

She went into the kitchen and closed the door firmly. Jumeau stood solemnly in the courtyard looking at his bicycle and musing silently to himself, "We will speak. We shall speak. We shall speak, *you* will speak." He felt that despite difficulties and lack of cooperation, he had acquitted himself well. He would enjoy describing the affair to his wife, though of course she would not understand all the nuances as she had no knowledge of English whatever.

Helen expressed herself to Rosemary with brief finality.

"He's a fool. Let's drop the subject for good." Rosemary was delighted to comply.

5 ALBERT ARRIVED HOME WHEN LUNCH WAS
almost over, cheerful and pink and shiny.

"I don't feel like much," he said. "A bite and some coffee and
a doss for a couple of hours."

"We always have a siesta," Rosemary explained. "It's too
hot to do anything else. French people all do it, you know."

"Oh?" Helen showed proper respect. She went out to the
courtyard to renew acquaintance with the little car and came
back in shaken.

"Somebody's scraped my fender!" she reported. Albert
wheeled round, slack-jawed.

"Which one?" He was too drunk to drive, of course. Helen
felt a furious anger at him. He must have brushed against
something. He had gone out to the yard and was kneeling
beside the scraped fender, feeling underneath it for damage.

"You must have done it when you brought it inside last
night," he blustered. "It's madness moving a car about in the
dark when you're not experienced."

"Really." Helen couldn't trust herself to discuss it. It was
silly. She despised people who were hypnotized by their pos-
sessions, the material values, the status-seekers. A car was
simply a machine. Nevertheless, she doted on the little car,
and a scratch, even a slight scratch, was a kind of defilement.

47

"It's nothing," Albert said. "It's only a retouch job. It could happen to anybody."

Helen kneeled and examined the scratch, which certainly didn't look fatal.

"I'll get it fixed for you," Albert promised her. "You'll never know it was touched."

"Yes." She went indoors and thought of other things. The family went upstairs to lie down and sleep off the weight of lunch and sunshine, and she lay down too. The scratch on the car nagged at her and spoiled her rest.

"This won't do," she muttered and got up and tiptoed downstairs so as not to disturb the house. She muttered to the engine to be silent as she started it and backed it out of the courtyard. The street was empty and dead, and it occurred to her that garages might be closed, but there was no harm in trying. She found the place without difficulty and drove into the yard. It was an untidy place with one petrol pump, several well-worn scooters and an old van standing on a ramp with the hood open. She got out and looked round, trying not to seem inquisitive in case somebody should see her.

A youth emerged from a dark doorway, in a gleaming white sports shirt and narrow trousers with a razor crease.

"Petrol?" he said, eyeing her casually. It must be the climate. People *did* eye you, as a matter of routine. Even that fatuous policeman.

"No," she said. "I have . . ." what was the word for "scratched"? She resorted to signs and pointed to the mark on the fender. The youth came over and examined it without enthusiasm.

"It's nothing."

"You can paint it?"

48

"Ah, it's nothing, why bother? We're very busy—" he waved his hand at the gray van. "This, you hardly notice it, it's not worth repairing."

A spineless little layabout, Helen diagnosed. She longed to tell him to stand up straight and get his hand out of his pocket.

"Where is M. Pennard?" she asked coldly.

"Ah, he's busy. Honestly, it's nothing, madame." This one didn't even have the instinct to know that she was mademoiselle. In his eyes I'm an old woman.

"Have the goodness to ask M. Pennard to speak to me," she said, and he looked sullen.

"Paul!" He turned his back on her and strolled over to the gray van and inspected the engine with deep concern. Helen was not impressed. Never done a hand's turn in his life, she decided—he knows no more about that engine than I do.

Pennard appeared in the doorway, once again in dungarees and sucking his teeth. Helen realized with remorse that he must have been at lunch, but his face lit up pleasantly when he saw her.

"Ah, mademoiselle!" He came across the yard and shook her hand. There was something pleasantly . . . convincing about him. The air of the skilled workman, she decided. She had a deep respect for skill and was easily irritated by incompetence. That's what they mean, she thought idly, by the solidarity of the Workers—not the solidarity of people who had jobs, but of people who worked efficiently and respected work. She pointed apologetically to the scratched fender, and Pennard said, "Ah, it is nothing."

He used the same words as the dandified youth, but where the youth had clearly meant, "It is nothing so forget it," Pen-

49

nard equally clearly meant, "It is nothing, we can fix it." He stooped to examine the scratch and said, "You must take better care of your pretty little child, mademoiselle."

Helen blushed and laughed. "You know what women drivers are."

"Ah, no, I was joking, simply. I respect women drivers."

"You mean you avoid them?"

Pennard smiled.

"No, I accept lifts from them."

"One must live dangerously."

"You speak French very very well, mademoiselle. You have spent much time in France."

"One day!"

"No kidding!"

"Yes," Helen said happily. "I learned at school. A very long time ago."

"Ah, not very long ago."

"You are too kind, monsieur." Helen laughed happily. This was the France she had pictured—a littered garage yard drowsing in the southern sunshine, far from the tourist spots, and an absurd conversation with a real French citizen, flattering comments on her fluency. It was a conversation such as she had rehearsed a hundred times in the gray stone house in Stirlingshire—*but how astonishing, mademoiselle, you must have lived for many years in France to speak so well.* That's what a good Scotch education does for you. She delighted in the easygoing, sexless rapport between herself and a garage mechanic.

"But I mustn't disturb you, monsieur, you must be very busy."

He shrugged.

"Perhaps I can come back? It will be finished today?"

"Without a doubt, mademoiselle." Pennard looked thoughtfully toward the immaculate youth. "I will put my assistant on to it."

"Ah, what a shame, monsieur—it will spoil his beautiful clothes."

Pennard grinned.

"I am a very cruel boss, eh? Oh, I detest myself."

"A wicked tyrant, monsieur, it's the truth." They laughed to each other. The solidarity of the workers uniting against the layabouts.

"Au revoir, then, monsieur."

"À bientôt, mademoiselle. Oh, an hour, two hours."

As she walked out of the yard she heard Pennard speaking to the dandified youth and the dandified youth raising his voice in sullen protest. From somewhere inside the house a petulant female voice called "Paul! Paul!" His mother?

Feeling light and free, Helen turned downhill toward the village. The land rose steeply from the sea, and the main village lay almost vertically below. There was a public square, laid out like a toy, with a circular concrete platform in the center, and beyond that a shopping street etched hard in sunlight, and beyond that, a confusion of rooftops and the long beach.

She felt irrationally that she was playing truant, and the thought made her both guilty and joyful. Rosemary and the family were, after all, sleeping and didn't need her. She picked her way down a steep serpentine path to sea level. The sun would blister her nose. She found a chemist's shop and bought sun-tan oil. She wandered along a shady arcade, staring in shop windows at familiar things with unfamiliar names. "En vente"? On the wind? No, "For Sale," of course. She had the arcade almost to herself so early in the afternoon. Its shade led the eye engagingly along the shop fronts splashed with sunlight, and she had a start of fear when she saw the only other window-shopper at the far end: a tall young man with bright fair hair, lounging gracefully and gazing at a shop window. It couldn't be a mistake; he was the beautiful young hitchhiker from Le Touquet. He turned and stared back, and there was no doubt at all. For a long moment she held his stare, unsure whether he could see her clearly as she stood in shadow. He didn't move. Involuntarily she began to back away. The figure, far away down the mottled corridor of the arcade, stood quite still, elegant and composed, and pregnant, she felt, with menace. She resisted a relapse into the drowning panic that had maddened her the night before. There was no reason, no real reason, to connect the beautiful young man with the prowler in the night. But she continued to back away.

The sleeping sunshine beauty of the village was destroyed abruptly. The quiet deserted street became a threat. She looked round slowly, praying for a crowd to appear. It was the childhood nightmare of fleeing along a long, straight street with the imperative need to find a turning and muscles thick and heavy. But I am not a child in a nightmare, she thought. I am an adult with a clear head, and there are people not far away, and nothing can happen in a sunlit street, even a deserted street. She had backed until she was standing beside a lane at the end of the row of shops. She turned and advanced slowly into it, as a woman might have advanced slowly into a shop door. Only when she was well out of sight of the arcade did she begin to hurry. She hurried in earnest.

Paul Pennard listened with evident sympathy to the plaints of Charles, his young brother-in-law. It was certainly true that one didn't want to be playing with paint in one's best shirt and trousers.

"Yes, it would be a pity to spoil your pretty clothes, Charles," he said. Charles, relieved, agreed, but Paul went on to say, "So you'd probably better change into something else."

"To paint that stupid little scratch?" Charles was incredulous.

"Sure thing." Paul picked up a wrench and started to crawl under the gray van.

"But it would only take you a few minutes, Paul," Charles pleaded. "I was going to try out the scooter."

"In your new clothes?"

Charles shook his head and kicked the ground.

Madame Robet came to the door and sized up the situation at once. Her instinct was to defend her handsome son and his beautiful new clothes, which were too good for menial work on some stranger's car, but Madame Robet was a strategist, and she tried to soothe young Charles into changing into old clothes for a few minutes and helping his brother-in-law.

"We must help one another, that's what families are for, Charles," she pleaded. "Can you not run Madeleine to the shop, Paul? Paul!"

Paul dragged himself out from under the gray van.

"She has plenty of time," he said. "I must get on with this."

"I thought you might run her to the shop," Madame Robet persisted. Madeleine appeared from the house behind her mother and shook her head quickly to silence the old woman, who glared at her.

The Pennard household consisted of Paul, his mother-in-law and her two children Madeleine and Charles. Paul was a widower of four years' standing, and his in-laws had imperceptibly become part of the ménage during his wife's illness.

Madame Robet, the widow of a minor civil servant, considered that she was doing her son-in-law a favor by managing his home and giving him the comfort of feminine management. It was an arrangement that was perfect for everybody. The garage business was not very aristocratic, but it made a living and made life easier than a widow's pension.

There was also the question of her children's future. Young Charles, at twenty-one, had never really settled. She had not been able to give him the education that would have fitted his abilities, and inevitably, he found it difficult to apply himself to the lowlier jobs that were open to him. The garage business would be a splendid insurance for Charles' future. It could be better, of course—selling new cars would be much more acceptable than repairing old broken vans. That would suit Charles, but Paul was lacking in ambition, and she had to keep coaxing Charles to seem enthusiastic about helping in the repair shop in the meantime so that Paul could be persuaded that he ought to improve his business. In Madame Robet's eyes, Charles' sullenness was only natural, the distaste of a well-bred young man for a dirty trade. But it exasperated her that Charles didn't have the sense to pretend more enthusiasm in the present.

Then there was Madeleine, pallid and resigned at twenty-eight, working in a greengrocer's and not even trying. God knew she was no great catch, but Paul was not a young man, and all that nonsense was behind him. Madeleine could cook and clean, and she would never give a husband any uneasy moments.

Madame Robet's situation was comfortable enough to keep her mind active in measures for safeguarding it, and she was shrewd enough to see that some men in Paul's position would not consider they had any obligations to the family of a dead wife. The important thing was to establish a more solid footing. A partnership for Charles, a convenient marriage between Paul and Madeleine, and the world would be solidly assured.

Madeleine, far from cooperating, positively shrank from too much friendliness with Paul. She stubbornly resisted her mother's intelligent stratagems to throw her and Paul together. And Paul, without seeming to resist, had simply shown no interest. It was a thing that had to be managed very subtly so as not to frighten him off.

Madame Robet would not have been happy to know how much Paul understood of her ambitions. He had divined them with private amusement before his wife was dead a week. Of his three in-laws, he preferred Madame Robet herself. The old lady was made of hard stuff and she was intent on survival. He almost admired this quality, and he sympathized with her, though he would never have insulted her by telling her. Besides, it was true that she could cook beautifully and keep his house comfortable even if it was a little crowded with her two children.

As far as her ambitions were concerned, Paul regarded them as the basis of a permanent war which he enjoyed because he couldn't take it seriously. He had no intention of marrying the pallid Madeleine, who was harmless and futile, and he had no intention of sharing his business with Charles, who was conceited and futile. In the meantime, he had the comfort of a tidy house, and Madeleine at least supported herself, and from time to time he could amuse himself by forcing Charles to work. He didn't do this very often because the effort was hardly worth it. Today, he was permitting himself the occasional luxury of being mean and brutal and insisting that

55

Charles should perform the tiny job of retouching the tourist woman's car. He smiled happily and wriggled under the van to loosen the sump bolts.

Charles, bitter and misunderstood, allowed his mother to induce him to change and look at the scratched fender. He fed his resentment by fetching water and washing the fender with unnecessary care and making the job as difficult and objectionable as possible. He ran a wet sponge along the underside and was perversely pleased at taking off a thick mud.

"Filthy!" he muttered with sour satisfaction. He decided to wash out all the mud from the underside. It was an act of flagellation. He lay down on his back in calculated discomfort and shoved the soaking sponge up into the fender. It was in doing this that he suddenly became interested in the small red car. The sponge should have slid smoothly along the dirt-caked surface, but it was interrupted by something harder than mere dirt. He refilled it with water and rubbed industriously. He looked at the topside of the fender and tried to calculate whether there could be any electrical equipment fastened underneath it, but there could be nothing apart from a few wires leading to the lamps—certainly nothing to account for what felt like a solid box. He lifted the hood and discovered four big boltheads that appeared to have no function at all. He tried a screwdriver on one but realized that this was useless unless one had a wrench with which to imprison the nuts on the other side of the metal.

"Have a look at this, Paul!" he shouted. Paul answered impatiently in a muffled voice from under the gray van.

"All right, to hell with you," Charles muttered. He lay on his back again and twisted the front wheel of the little car so that he could peer up into the fender. There appeared to be a metal box growing out from one side of it. It had eight screwheads round the edges.

Although he was immensely uninterested in tinkering with dirty machinery, Charles was intensely interested in cars themselves, and this was something quite unusual in any car. An idea was growing joyfully in Charles' mind. He found a screwdriver and started to unscrew the cover of the metal box. The screws turned smoothly and easily, and he laid them meticulously on the ground beside him. Then he gripped the cover of the box and pulled it off.

There were no wires inside. The box appeared to be full of foam rubber. Puzzled, he slid the screwdriver up inside one edge and found that the rubber could be pulled out in one piece, apparently a solid block of stuff. As he straightened up, he found that it was rubber foam which had been pressed hard into the shape of the box. It was not one piece but two horizontal layers, and when he lifted off the top one, he found himself staring at several rows of translucent pebbles embedded in the foam.

From the moment of discovering the box, Charles had immediately thought of smuggling. It was the perfect dodge for concealing something small and valuable.

"What's the trouble?" Paul shouted.

Charles started. "O.K., it's all right," he called back. Paul started to wriggle under the gray van again. What could you smuggle into France? That was the question. Charles had no doubt it was diamonds. He tried to remember whether diamonds were cheaper in England than in France, but, obviously, they must be, or there was no point in bringing them. His hands were trembling, and he worked with frantic haste to lift the pebbles from the rubber foam and slip them into a pocket before Paul or his mother could turn up and become curious. One of the pebbles rolled right under the little red car, and he gave a little moan of horror, but there was no time to recover it; he was desperate to pack the rubber foam back into the box under the fender and screw the lid back into place.

He sweated with tension as he pressed the lid into place and tried to run the first screw home. It was a job that needed three hands—one to hold the lid, one to hold the screw and one to hold the screwdriver. The screw fell and rolled out of sight, and he sobbed and cursed. No matter, it didn't need all eight screws. He was limp by the time he managed to engage another screw in one of the holes and run it home. The rest were easier. He sat up and mopped his brow.

First he must recover the pebble that had rolled under the car. There were over sixty of the things, but he had convinced himself that every single one was vital. If the missing one were found lying there, it would give the game away. He lay on his stomach and peered under the car and cursed. The surface of the ground was dust and pebbles, and the lost stone was lost in perfect camouflage. He combed the dust with sensitive fingers, gathering pebbles with loving caution. Yes, this was the one; it must be the one.

"Are you digging for gold?" Paul asked him. Paul was standing beside him, looking down wearily, damn him. Charles stood up awkwardly with a handful of dust and the pebble.

"I dropped a franc," he complained. Paul was shaking his head.

"Ah, Charles," he said, "everything is against you."

"I'd better wash my hands," Charles muttered. He hurried into the house and went straight to his bedroom. There was no time for clever concealment. He emptied the stones into the little box where he kept his cuff links and tiepins and pushed it to the back of a drawer. Then he washed his hands and face and went out to the yard. He was sure he was walking strangely; his leg muscles appeared to have forgotten the trick of walking. He rummaged to find a color to match the paintwork of the red car, and sweat kept running into his eyes. When he kneeled to apply the paint pencil to the fender, his hand shook till he had to grip his right wrist with his left hand and press hard on the fender to control it.

"It's the wrong color," Paul said from behind him. Charles looked round in terror at the sound of the voice, and a blob of paint splashed onto the fender.

"What's wrong, Charlot?" Paul laid a hand on his shoulder. "Are you ill?"

"It's my stomach," Charles muttered. "I'll be all right." Paul was gently prizing the paint pencil out of his hand.

"No, no, I'll do it, Charlot," he said. "You're shaking."

"No, honestly, I want to help, Paul. It's all right. I want to do my share—that's what families are for. . . ." His face muscles had developed minds of their own. Paul put a hand under his elbow and forced him gently to rise.

"Yes, well, we can't work if we're ill. Leave it, I'll do it. You can give me a hand tomorrow."

"Right, I'll do that, Paul, I swear it, I'll give you a hand tomorrow." Charles walked weakly into the house. He wanted to get away, but it would look funny if he went away after complaining of his stomach. Most of all he wanted to look in the drawer and make sure nothing had happened to the stones. He wedged a chair under the door handle and opened the little box. Perhaps they weren't diamonds. They didn't look like anything in particular. If they were diamonds, they would cut glass—but perhaps that was only after they were cut to a sharp edge. He took one to the window and rubbed it tentatively on the glass at one corner. There was no mark. He tried again, pressing harder, and a faint roughness appeared. He stared at it and wheeled back to the box. Grunting to himself, he started to scoop them up and weigh them in his hands. Then he began to count them. He counted them ten times. There were sixty-three. Sixty-three. He laughed at himself in the mirror. He counted them again.

He kicked off his shoes and lay on his back on the bed, with hands clasped behind his head. He jumped up in a panic and closed the box and put it back in the drawer. Then he took it out and counted them once more. He replaced the box in the drawer and went back to lie on the bed again, smiling dreamily. His smile faded and a look of deep concentration appeared on his face. What was he going to do now?

Helen was breathless when she slipped into the garage yard, and she found Paul kneeling beside her car gently rubbing the scratch.

"Eh, mademoiselle. Ça va?"

"Yes," she said weakly. "I climbed the hill too fast."

"Life is too short for hurrying." He noticed that she threw a glance over her shoulder and sidled round the wall. She was nervous as well as breathless. It was none of his business.

"I'm sorry, mademoiselle. My assistant has used the wrong color." Helen nodded without looking at the car. "I don't have the exact color," Paul went on, "I'll have to get it for you. Tomorrow, perhaps."

Helen sat on a box and nodded again, and after a curious glance, Paul turned away tactfully to wipe the fender. Helen realized he was preparing to hand the car over to her, and she didn't want to be dismissed.

"There's something else," she said quickly. "I don't know

what it is—something in the engine. It sort of . . ." Her French failed her. "It goes *Rrrrr* instead of *Ooooo*." Paul raised his eyebrows. "I'm sorry," she said, "I can't explain it very well." She glanced at the open gateway.

She looked, Paul thought, very feminine, with her cheeks flushed and her hair blown. He had taken her for a cool English miss, amiable and rather precise. Pink and out of breath, she had a tremendous quality that made her immensely more interesting. For some reason she didn't want to leave. He was curious.

"Would you like to drive the car?" he asked. "I'll sit beside you and listen to the *Rrrrr*."

"Yes! No . . . you drive, monsieur. I'm still a little upset."

Paul spread newspapers over the driving seat and got in. Helen thankfully sat in the passenger seat and rubbed her forehead, keeping her head bowed as the car was backed out of the yard. She was conscious that he was changing gear rapidly up and down.

"No *Rrrrr* yet," he muttered. He turned a corner sharply and opened out on a straight road. She looked up and saw that they were clear of the village and running along the high road above the coast. He stopped and switched off the engine.

"No *Rrrrrr*," he said.

"I'm sorry, monsieur. I have wasted your time."

"A poor man is rich in time."

She turned to him gratefully and kept turning so that she could see the road behind. There was no sign of life of any kind on it. For a moment she was tempted to tell this little French stranger about her absurd cloak-and-dagger fantasy, because here, in the open country and sitting beside the extremely practical and real Monsieur Pennard, she decided it *was* a fantasy. But her sense of proportion and propriety

61

stopped her. It was a compliment to offer conversation to a stranger. To offer him your troubles was discourtesy at least.

"Cigarette, mademoiselle?"

"No, thank you. Oh. Yes, would you mind? It's a new experience." She puffed at the dark tobacco conscientiously, and when Pennard opened his door and stepped out, she followed him.

"This is a luxury," he commented. "People who live here never have time to look at the view."

"It's wonderful."

"You don't find the sunshine too hot."

"No, I love it. I could live in the sun all the time. Are you sure I'm not wasting your time, monsieur?"

"Is it wasting time to stand in the sunshine with a pretty girl?"

"Thank you, monsieur."

"Ah!" he cried in surprise. "I was sure you would say 'nonsense' or 'flatterer'! I believed that an Englishwoman could never accept a compliment."

"I am not English, monsieur, I am Scots."

"Ah."

"A much superior race."

"Naturally, mademoiselle."

They laughed together.

"And therefore, thank you for the compliment." She looked out over the sea, still deep and smooth and vanishing into haze to the north.

She wasn't a pretty girl, in fact. Her mouth was too wide, and her nose was rather flat, and her skin was sallow. Still, he didn't feel he had offended the truth very seriously. Her eyes were big, and as she stood looking out to sea, he noticed how her back rose from the waist in a fine pliant curve.

62

Pleasant to touch with the eye. She had an atmosphere of firmness that he found agreeable, almost like a man. But there was nothing wrong with her car engine.

"An odd thing happened today, Monsieur Pennard." She had come to a decision on impulse, but she tried to make it sound amusing.

"Oh?"

"You remember the young man who asked me for a lift in Le Touquet?"

"Ah, yes."

"I saw him today in Saint-Tombe. In fact, I thought he was trying to follow me."

"Ah, Frenchmen . . ."

"No, honestly, I didn't mean that. I was quite . . . I mean, he didn't seem to be following me like *that*."

"For what reason, then?"

"Oh, I don't know." She got into the driving seat, and he shrugged and sat in the seat beside her. She started the car and turned it back toward the village. She had hoped he might be interested enough to press her with questions, but this was a man who didn't start conversations; he simply accepted them. She regretted having sounded foolish.

"I don't know," she said, not looking at him as she drove. "It doesn't matter—women often imagine that men are following them."

"Oh?"

"Yes, I mean, many women do." She was more and more sorry she had spoken.

"Are you that kind of woman, mademoiselle?"

"I don't know." She tried to laugh lightly. "Women of a certain age, you know . . ."

"Are you a woman of a certain age?"

"I'm thirty-four."

That was interesting. He wouldn't have trusted a guess. "That isn't a certain age, mademoiselle."

"Thank you very much." She drove on in silence.

"What you mean, mademoiselle—"

"Um?"

"I don't express myself well. What you mean is that women of a certain age are accused of imagining things, perhaps?"

"Ah, Monsieur Pennard, you're very good for the morale."

"But in any case, you are not a woman of a certain age."

"You express yourself most eloquently, I assure you." She laughed without effort. "Well, here we are."

She stopped in front of Rosemary's house. Vanessa was in the courtyard, and she shouted with joy and ran out to the car.

"I'll let you know when I have paint for your car, mademoiselle," said Pennard, and Helen was apologetic at once.

"But of course, monsieur, I'll drive you back to the garage."

"Not worth the trouble, mademoiselle."

"I insist. I'll be back in a few minutes, Vanessa."

"Can I came too, Aunt Helen?"

"Better not, this time—you'll have to tell your mummy I was here."

"All right." The little girl didn't complain, but she stepped back, looking wistful as the car moved away again.

"Your niece."

"Yes, she's an amiable little girl."

"She adores you."

"Oh?" Helen blushed. "You have sharper eyes than mine, monsieur."

"Perhaps." He smiled to himself. She stopped outside his yard, and he held the door open after he climbed out.

64

"All the same," he said, "I hope you're not worried about that man—the one who was following you?"

"No, it's nothing. Even I, I can imagine things."

"Be careful, all the same, mademoiselle."

"You're very kind, monsieur."

A middle-aged Frenchwoman, in black, had appeared from the yard, and was staring impatiently at Pennard's back.

"You were gone a long time, Paul," she said acidly. "Evidently you haven't much work to do."

"Not to worry, maman," he said easily, amused. "This lady is also a customer." Helen was oddly relieved that he was so self-assured, so unruffled, by the old lady. It would have been sad if he had cringed or apologized. The Frenchwoman snorted.

"These English tourists," she said in rapid French. "They'll chase after anybody—even a mechanic." Helen laughed in delight and said as rapidly as she could, "He isn't too ugly for a mechanic, madame."

If the old lady was dismayed that she had been understood, she didn't twitch.

"He'll be glad to know it, mademoiselle," she retorted and marched back into the yard.

"I'm sorry, Monsieur Pennard, I didn't mean to offend her."

"Ah!" He waved the suggestion away.

"Still," Helen persisted, "mothers are easily offended."

He shrugged.

"Madame is my mother-in-law."

"Even more so, then."

Pennard smiled.

"I'll get the paint as quickly as I can. Au revoir, mademoiselle."

"Au revoir, monsieur."

It was true, Helen decided, as she had always suspected—it was easier to be talkative in French than in English, even when your French stumbled here and there. Somehow the effort of using the strange language had the effect of by-passing normal shyness. Don't make a big thing of that, she thought—when were you so shy in English? Still, everything had a different flavor in French.

Or maybe I'm like a piano bore who learns "Chopsticks" and wants to play it all day long, she thought. She felt cheated at returning to the family and relapsing into drab old English. Vanessa gave her a rapturous welcome, certainly.

"Was that your boy friend, Aunt Helen?" she asked.

"Are you jealous, Vanessa?" Helen tugged the little girl's hair.

"No, no! He's nice." Her face was so woebegone that Helen laughed and squeezed her.

"Your aunt Helen's too old for boy friends," she assured her, and Vanessa squealed, "No, you're not!"

Rosemary wasn't nearly as rapturous.

"Where did you get to?" She was still blinking from sleep and her lipstick was half rubbed off. "I hope you're not going to make a habit of . . . just *vanishing*."

"I haven't thought about it yet."

The direct riposte always flummoxed Rosemary. Given an evasive apology, she could get properly warmed up, but she couldn't work out the next remark from this. Helen saw her difficulty and tried to help.

"I took the car to have the scratch painted over, that's all."

"Well!" Rosemary was still fumbling for the next assault. But Albert came hurrying out from the kitchen in indignation.

"I told you I would get it fixed! Now, no! Just listen to me, you don't know anything about cars, they're my business." He started to emphasize by chopping the air with the edge of his hand. "And I don't want you putting that car into any tuppence-hapenny French garage to get it beggared about by some ninny. I told you I would take care of it."

"If I feel inclined, Albert," Helen assured him, "I'll drive my car over a cliff. And I won't ask your permission."

"What are you talking about?" Albert was perfectly bewildered. "I got it for you, didn't I? What do you know about cars?"

Rosemary finally found her cue and joined in with something soothing.

"Now you know you don't know anything about them, Helen. You really must admit Albert knows best."

"Does it ever occur to you," Helen asked very gently, "to belt up?" Rosemary's reaction to this coarseness was so dramatic that Helen started to giggle. Albert had already stamped out into the street to sneer at the workmanship of a lousy French garage, but he hardly had time to look at the scratch. He was stooping beside the car and feeling tremulously inside the fender. His breath exploded in a gasp of relief.

"They've made a proper ass of it anyway," he proclaimed. "I warned you."

"They didn't have a matching color," Helen told him coolly. "It'll have to be done again. Monsieur Pennard's going to let me know."

Rosemary made a little grim nod of satisfaction.

"Wheels within wheels," she said to Albert, and then, "Could *that* be the attraction?" she asked Helen, with nauseating coyness.

67

"Ha, ha!" Albert shook. "Don't tell me you're deserting me for a Froggy, Helen!"

"For the love of Mike," Helen said. "He's simply a garagiste. And he's married, in case you're interested."

"Oh."

"Ah, don't kid yourself, Nellie." Albert was nearly his suave idiot self again. "The married ones are the worst."

"Uhuh." Helen was weary of this well-worn assurance. "How about a cup of tea?"

"That's a good idea!"

Families were really fantastic. After all this nagging, people ought to flounce out of one another's lives as mortal enemies and never darken the doormats again. A few minutes ago, Helen realized, she had felt on the point of doing that exactly. But it wasn't in her nature to flounce out of anything. And what you did instead was have a cup of tea and carry on as if nothing had happened at all. Still, even if it's true, she thought, it's damned silly. Strangers would never be so cheeky to one another. Families are a form of self-indulgence in bad manners. Especially Rosemary with her wheels within wheels and her offensive nonsense about boy friends. Rosemary had been quite deflated by the news that Pennard was married.

Helen lit the gas under the kettle and accepted the hard exercise of admitting that she too had been quite deflated by the news. It's a generalized Thing, of course, she reminded herself. You don't have any particular interest in any man *qua* man, but it would probably be very nice if every one of them was available. In that generalized sense. I mean, if you even have a mild friendly conversation with a total stranger and you know you'll never see him again in your entire life, it adds a . . . a fillip, if you like, if you know that something could come of it—in theory, that's all. If you know that—in that generalized sense—he's, um, well, *eligible*.

To her horror, she blushed all over.

6 MADAME ROBET WAS WORRIED ABOUT YOUNG
Charles. She was worried about Charles most of the time, but
now she had something specific as a focus for the worry.
She was standing in the kitchen, feeding hare and pork into
the mincing machine in small pieces, to get them mixed
properly from the start, and calculating the heat of the oven
with another part of her mind, and counting how many to-
matoes she would have to disembowel and whether she would
make onion soup after all.

And she was wondering about Charles. He was looking
pale and nervous, and he was even more evasive than usual.
He had refused her medicine and lurked silently in the house
after lunch, and then he had suddenly decided to test the
repaired scooter and disappeared like a racing driver. Either
he was up to some devilment with that Louis and his crowd of
no-good hooligans, or he was mixed up with some girl. If anything, the possibility of some minor crime was preferable to
a misadventure with a predatory woman. Young women nowadays had no shame in the way they threw themselves at
men—older women were even worse, for that matter.

It was a long time since Madame Robet had considered
throwing herself at any man, and in her considered opinion,
such things should now come to an end entirely. She called

70

out of the window to Paul, who was lying on his back like any common laborer, working underneath the butcher's van.

"Where has Charles taken that scooter, Paul?"

"I don't know."

"Nobody ever knows anything."

Paul sat up.

"I thought he was sick," he shouted. "He must have made a quick recovery."

Paul, she realized, had no sympathy with Charles. Probably the boy *was* sick, and he had gone out to get some fresh air rather than complain. That was how she would put it to anybody else, but she knew Charles well enough to be sure that he was more likely up to something stupid. But it wouldn't do to express a suspicion like that to Paul. He wasn't in the family, after all, and it would do him no good to imagine that any Robet could be less than perfect. She decided that they would have onion soup after all. It would keep her mind occupied.

Young Charles, in fact, wasn't too sure himself what he was up to. He had spent an hour with his brain fairly boiling while he considered what to do with the sixty-three little pebbles in his drawer. He had dismissed any doubts as to what they were—they *must* be diamonds. This meant that, in a sense, he was a millionaire. He would never have to repair another flat as long as he lived. He would have a Mercedes 200 SL . . . or perhaps even a Facel Vega. No, a Vega was too big and middle-aged. A Mercedes or a Thunderbird. Or an Alfa Romeo? And if he ever blew a tire, some peasant in a garage would have the trouble of repairing it.

Ideally, he would leave home and have an apartment of his own—not in Saint-Tombe, by God, but in Paris. The snag was that his mother would never let him leave home. Even in his fevered imagination he couldn't visualize her simply wishing him luck and saying good-bye. And then, Bettine was in Saint-Tombe. But maybe she would come to Paris if he was a millionaire? Not to get married, that was strictly for the birds. Well, never mind Paris for the moment, he could surely get what he wanted from Bettine if he had money to flash. A few thousand francs would sweep away her stubborn grasp on her chastity. He almost hated Bettine as he thought of how persistently she resisted him. It would serve the bitch right if he produced some other bit—something with blond hair and long legs and high breasts, an American even. You could get women like that if you were loaded.

The difficulty that kept beating in his brain, however, was the prime difficulty that he didn't have any money at all. He only had a boxful of uncut diamonds, hot property, and he realized that his education lacked any practical value, because he had no idea how to sell hot diamonds. It was the kind of thing the boys would sometimes discuss, with careless confidence, and he always sounded as confident as any, but when you got right down to it, where did you do it? Fences didn't have advertisements in the papers or plates outside their doors. And even if there was a fence in Saint-Tombe, this was big-time stuff. It called for a big operator.

And then, if you found a fence, he would try to cheat you. Especially if you looked young and inexperienced. Just let him try it! Charles clenched his fists and visualized himself beating a smirking receiver to a pulp. He discovered he was trembling with rage.

There was always a chance that Louis might know somebody—Louis always gave the impression that he knew everything. But this was too big for Louis too. Anyway, the important thing was not to let anybody else in on it. Louis hadn't found the stuff, had he? Louis was too damned smart for his own good. He would recede to his proper importance when he, Charles, was a millionaire. But let's not be too showy about it—we don't want anybody asking questions. The scheme is to keep the money well tucked away and just use it very gradually . . . and then pretend to have found a job in Paris and scoot, vanish. Cannes, Nice—Majorca, all the American tourists went to Majorca nowadays. You could live it up there, and nobody would have any reason to be suspicious.

All this merely increased the hideous feeling of urgency and helplessness. He had to do something or go insane. When he heard Paul leave with the Englishwoman, he made up his mind.

There was no question of taking the whole collection of stones anywhere. It terrified him even to have them in his drawer, without a two-foot lead sheathing round it. He examined them again and picked out the very smallest. This, with fiendish cunning, he wrapped in a scrap of cloth and put into a matchbox and then laid matches on top of it. By this ruse, even if he were in an accident with the scooter, nobody would discover anything. The chance of an accident with the scooter brought the sweat sizzling down the small of his back. He would simply have to be careful.

At least it was all ready to take out, and it started easily. To his disgust, his mother appeared just as he was driving out of the yard, but he couldn't trust himself to speak to anybody. He gunned the motor to drown any remarks, waved to her, and roared out into the street and drove for Dinard like a rocket.

It stood to reason that there must be somebody genuinely dishonest—criminally dishonest—in a town like Dinard, with tourists pouring through by the thousand. It was an obvious place for rackets. He forgot his resolution to take care on the road. The situation was too desperate for dillydallying. Speed helped to calm his nerves, in any case. He was able to think more clearly and work out possible stratagems while he was pelting along at a good sixty-five.

In Dinard, he searched for a convenient place to park the scooter first. It had to be handy and ready to start and away from busy streets in case he needed to leave in a hurry, but it couldn't be too far away. Then he started to walk through the streets in search of a likely-looking jeweler.

The accursed tourists were everywhere. In a way, crowds were a comfort, but they made it certain that any jeweler's shop would be mobbed with people, and he needed a perfectly empty shop. He stopped miserably outside several places with watches and rings in the window and stared in the windows and into the shops. There was always some client inside, and when finally he found one that was momentarily empty, he convinced himself that the man at the counter would be a mere clerk with no idea about anything and no wit or money.

The strain of doing nothing was exhausting him. He went into a café and drank coffee in an effort to cool down and regain his confidence. Then he left the busy streets and began to comb the quiet little places where, after all, a crooked jeweler was more likely to have his headquarters. Not that he necessarily needed a crook. No, it was too risky—he could more easily set about finding a proper fence when he had some money and some time to think. What was needed in the meantime was a real jeweler who would believe his story and have enough money to pay for one very small diamond. If crooked, all the better. If honest, no harm done.

He finally found the place on the shady side of a narrow little street. R. Vauban. It was a clean enough place, but small, with only one window, and rather shabby. And more important, it was perfectly empty. He went in, and an old-fashioned bell clanged as he closed the door.

The man behind the counter was thick-set and middle-aged. He looked somewhat ill-natured, but he was actually looking at a dismantled wristwatch with a jeweler's eyeglass screwed into his face, and this convinced Charles that he had come to the right kind of place.

"I can't take any more repairs, I'm absolutely snowed under," the man said truculently.

"I don't want a repair."

The man's attitude changed at once, and he laid the eyeglass on the counter and put on a pair of rimless spectacles. Oddly enough, they made him look rather formidable. Charles tried to smile confidently.

"I would like you to value something for me."

"I don't buy secondhand watches." The man's attitude soured again.

"No, no," Charles said and added "I'm not proposing to sell anything" in the hope of establishing a better atmosphere. The man gave him no encouragement whatever. He pulled the matchbox out of his pocket and carefully extracted the stone wrapped in cloth.

"This has been in the family for donkey's years," he explained. "My father got it as a keepsake, and I've had it since he died. It suddenly occurred to me that it might be worth something—not much, probably. Still, one was curious . . ."

"Oh?"

The man took the stone, with evident apathy, weighed it in his hand and kept looking at Charles instead of the stone.

"What do you think it is?" he asked. Charles found himself flushing.

"How do I know? Still . . . I'm not an expert . . ."

"Evidently."

The jeweler held the stone up to the light, took off his spectacles and examined it through the little eyeglass. Charles rested his hands on the counter, where they left damp images of themselves. His wrists prickled at the sudden thought of fingerprints. He tried unobtrusively to move his fingertips back and forth to smudge the marks. The jeweler abruptly walked into the back shop, out of sight, and Charles had an overpowering impulse to flee. His ears strained for the sound of a telephone. Of course—he had been a fool to let the thing out of his sight. The man would be calling the police at this very moment. His legs were paralyzed with fright, but he had the presence of mind to take out his handkerchief and wipe the marks of his hands off the counter. He was not such an amateur, he thought, and the thought restored his courage slightly.

The man came out of the back shop.

"Where did you say you got this?"

Now Charles had only one desire, and that was to get the stone back into his own possession.

"I noticed it looked funny against the light," he stammered. "Like this." He reached out his hand for the stone, and the jeweler, after a moment's hesitation, gave it to him. Charles held it up toward the shop door. "It looks . . . rather curious. I thought it might be . . . " his voice tailed off.

"Where did you get it?"

"I told you, I got it among my father's things when he died."

"It might be worth something," the jeweler said in a rather disagreeable tone. "Where did your father pick it up?"

"I . . . how do I know? He traveled a lot. I suppose it's

76

worthless, really. I was just curious and I happened to be passing . . ."

"Oh, I might offer you . . . fifty francs for it. It isn't of much value." The jeweler's tone was still contemptuous, but Charles' senses sharpened like a ferret's. Fifty francs, oh yes, and then quietly cut it up and make a thousand—ten thousand, perhaps! It was too glib.

"No . . . I don't think I'll bother—it has more sentimental value, I suppose. . . ."

"It might be worth a little more. If you give me your name I'll look into it."

"No, no, I wouldn't trouble you, I was simply curious."

The jeweler was staring hard at him.

"Let me have another look at it," he said. Charles slipped the stone into his jacket pocket with clammy fingers.

"No, no, it's not worth the trouble, I've decided not to sell it—my mother wouldn't approve, in any case . . ."

"Let's have another look at it." The jeweler sounded hard and domineering, and Charles stepped back from the counter.

"It's not worth the trouble, I assure you . . . I'll think about it. Yes, I'll think about it—perhaps I'll come back. I—I'll discuss it with my mother."

"You could leave it with me for a proper examination." The jeweler held out his hand, and Charles knew for certain that the man was as big a liar as himself.

"No, thanks. I'll think about it." He started toward the door.

"Just a minute! You never got that from your father! Stay where you are, lad!"

Charles opened the door and stepped briskly into the street, waving his hand in refusal, to keep up the fiction as long as possible. But the instant he was outside, he ran. The jeweler

77

shouted after him, but he kept running. He was almost sure the jeweler had started after him, but he was sure the heavy middle-aged man would never catch him—as long as other people didn't get curious. He threw himself round a corner, and then another, and then another and slowed down to a brisk walk before he dared to look back. He was perspiring all over. In less than a minute he had emerged on a busy street crowded with strollers, and he stopped to mop his brow and curse himself.

Clearly, the jeweler had been no fool—but he hadn't necessarily been a stool pigeon either. If Charles had had the guts to face up to him and play it tough, the man would probably have agreed to some arrangement. He had probably lost his chance. He couldn't go back now, in case the jeweler was a law-abiding citizen—he might have called the police already! Charles hurried to the street where he had parked the scooter and started back to Saint-Tombe cursing savagely.

He was actually in Saint-Tombe, a bare half mile from home, when he took a corner too fast. The scooter slid outward from under him, and he found himself poised, horizontal, a foot above the road, spinning forward very slowly and thinking very quickly that this time he would probably die. Then the ground came up in a blur to meet him and everything ceased.

7

THE CHILDREN WERE IN A MOOD OF FRETFUL
expectancy, which Helen could easily understand. They lived,
she decided, a dreary, uneventful life in a family in which the
only thing that ever happened was that something new was
bought. Albert was fond of them as long as they didn't make
a nuisance of themselves, and Rosemary felt that she had
made the final sacrifice by giving birth to them and allowing
them into such a well-heeled household. This diagnosis, Helen
admitted to herself, was too glib and sweeping, but it had
some of the truth, and she sensed that Roddy and Vanessa
had turned to her in the vague hope that a stranger would
provide stimulation and excitement.

That was the whole trouble with child-rearing in the af-
fluent society, she mused for the hundredth time. People were
so wrapped up with money and cars and refrigerators that
they expected children to be satisfied with the same things.
They smothered their kids with money to save themselves the
necessity of smothering them with attention and then were
surprised when the kids kept wanting more.

She was turning into a reactionary philosopher, she suspected. But what can you expect of a schoolmarm? The
teacher had to supply the patience and the interest that parents don't seem to be willing to give any longer. It was an

old staff room tirade of Helen's, and she often wished she could compel parents to be present when she was on her hobbyhorse. When she had two parents ready to hand in Albert and Rosemary, of course, she found that it was impossible to say a word on the subject. Parents had a way of looking knowing and indulgent when a spinster said anything about bringing up children. The act of procreation had infused them with a mystical wisdom that no outsider could ever achieve.

The only thing she could do in the circumstances was to carry on being a sucker and giving the kids her own time. It wasn't too much of a chore, she found. She was strongly drawn to pallid little Vanessa, and even Roddy with his sullen hostility could be a more stimulating companion than Albert or Rosemary. She offered to take the children away by themselves on a picnic.

"Are you sure you feel all right?" Rosemary asked, and Helen instantly answered, "No, maybe you're right—I could have a nap instead, and you can take the kids down to the beach."

It disposed of Rosemary's insinuations at once. She assured Helen that an outing with the kids was probably just what she needed.

"It'll give me peace to do some shopping," she added, and Albert groaned theatrically.

"Oh, oh! That's the way the money goes!" Rosemary sniffed at him.

Roddy was still slightly suspicious of the idea of going on an expedition with his soppy little sister and a soppy female aunt. Having discovered that Helen was a schoolteacher, he felt compelled to despise her even more. Helen disposed of his hostility by candidly offering to leave him behind. On an obscure impulse to reduce her femininity for his benefit, she changed into dark cotton slacks and a blouse, and was rewarded with an approving whoop and a pat on the buttocks from Albert. Rosemary regarded this childishness with weary indulgence. Men couldn't help it; it was a reflex action. Helen, she admitted to herself, could wear slacks without looking ghastly like some women—she didn't bulge across the back. But she was nothing to create any excitement, little hard buttocks like a boy's. Rosemary found reassurance in regarding Helen's figure because to Rosemary it had an unconscious quality—Helen didn't have too much of anything, and she seemed to be unaware of having anything at all. She had absolutely no idea. To underline the point in her own mind, Rosemary went indoors and changed into short, tight shorts and a blouse with a frilly front. Helen thought she looked a little excessive, but Albert responded by patting his own wife's bottom and would have squeezed her if Rosemary hadn't given him one of her sinking looks.

"You can take the Cresta, Helen," Albert offered grandly. "You'll need it with the kids. Rosemary and I'll have the Dodgem."

Helen bridled at once. It was all very well for Albert to swap cars around as if they were saucepans, but she didn't regard hers as a saucepan. This problem was solved by the wails of Roddy and Vanessa, who were blasé about driving in a vast machine and thought the Mini was a jollier toy.

"O.K., O.K." Albert gave in with rather bad grace. "Just watch how you drive, you know what French drivers are like."

Rosemary cut in testily. "I've already explained all that to Helen. How many traveler's checks have you got on you?"

"Here we go!" Albert gave a complacent impersonation of a henpeck. "Stay off the booze, Helen, eh?"

"I'll try," Helen assured him dryly, and the children started to scramble over each other into the little red car.

"It's not very big, is it?" Roddy persisted in withholding his enthusiasm.

"It's *lovely!*" Vanessa shrieked.

"Our car can go at eighty," he sneered. Helen gunned the engine and let the clutch out with a bang, to jolt him back in his seat. Vanessa squealed in delight.

"It's like a racer!"

"Our car can do eighty," Roddy insisted.

"Can't, it can't! Mummy doesn't let it! See!"

"This car can do eighty-five," Helen said calmly.

"Huh! I don't think!"

Helen changed up and rammed her foot down. The little car surged ahead, and Roddy's eyes went sideways so that he could stare at the speedometer without seeming to.

"Anybody could drive a car as little as this," he muttered defensively.

Berry was at the wheel of the big Citroën this time. Step by step, Berry's impatient lust for action had won over Laurent's caution. Berry was in a tight, ugly temper after setting out to tail Helen and then losing her in the village. He no longer merely wanted to get his hands on the goods, he wanted to hurt somebody in the process, Helen for preference. Laurent, acutely sensitive because of his own timidity, had refrained from scoffing at his rash young partner. He felt more and more that he had started something he couldn't control, and he was developing the suspicion that Berry was quite capable of turning on him if he gave him half a chance.

"We'll finish this off today!" Berry snarled to himself, as he swung the Citroën out of a side turning and rolled after the little red car.

"Sure, sure, you're right. A nice quiet snatch and then we're away." Laurent tried to sound friendly and approving.

"Nice quiet snatch!" Berry was hardly aware of Laurent's presence. He gripped the wheel savagely and swore to himself to relieve his feelings. "Damned bitch, I'll teach that one a lesson. Bitch bitch bitch."

"Yes." Laurent slumped in misery.

"I know what she wants!"

"A nice quiet snatch." Laurent too was talking to himself, to soothe his nerves. "And then away. I think I'll buy a restaurant. A restaurant would be nice."

"She doesn't know what's coming to her! She's in for a treat, that one, and she doesn't know it!"

"Not one of those big places, somewhere quiet, just a few tables."

"Have you ever had an English bit, Laurent?"

"No." Laurent slumped lower and his eyes glazed over with the sickness of despair.

Helen had resumed control of her childishness, and was refusing to boot the little car up to eighty-five. Instead, she had induced Vanessa to continue with the French lesson, and the little girl was yelling "un, deux, trois" with quivering fervor.

"French is soppy," Roddy opined.

"If you don't take the French lesson, I won't give you the diving lessons," Helen told him.

"Diving? *You* can't dive!"

"She can too!" Vanessa shouted. "She can dive lovely. You can't even swim."

83

"Neither can you, smarty, and shut your mouth or I'll belt you!"

"Can't you swim, Roddy?" Helen asked, astonished.

"So what? I'm only ten. And I don't believe you can dive."

"You'll learn to swim today. And so will Vanessa," Helen promised them grimly. "It's absolutely ridiculous not being able to swim."

Vanessa crowed with joy, but after brooding for a few moments, Roddy remarked uncertainly, "You can't teach me to swim, I'm too heavy."

"Nobody is too heavy."

"I just sink. I'm not like other people."

"You'll float today!" Helen's tone was menacing and final, and he chewed this threat over.

"I don't believe you can dive," he said, but he did believe it. Helen felt strong and useful and in control. Kids were an unconscionable pest, but they brought you back to sanity. Almost without thinking about it, she found she had thrown off the nagging sense of worry that had discolored the last two days.

If Berry had known about this lifting of Helen's spirits, he would have been delighted. He was rolling her over lusciously in his mind as an imaginative cat might roll a mouse, and it added to his pleasure that she could have no inkling of what was in store for her. What was in store for her was quite specific and anatomical. Berry too felt strong and purposeful, and secret, a completely unseen and unsuspected force closing in on a completely unseeing and unsuspecting victim.

"She's got kids with her," Laurent remarked timidly.

"All the better. I mean, so what?"

"Nothing."

They were probably heading for a beach. A nice small deserted beach. The English bit was the kind that would be nervous of appearing in a bathing suit with other people watching. Better and better. The shyer the better.

Helen stopped in the first village to buy fruit and lemonade. It was a small place with only half a dozen shops, but every one seemed to specialize in enormous canoes and air beds and skin-diving stuff. Roddy wanted to buy it all. Helen found, however, that if she simply ignored his demands, he forgot them. He wanted sweets and not soppy apples.

"You eat too many sweets," she told him.

"I've got money of my own!"

"O.K.," she said, "if you buy sweets for yourself, you get none of this stuff."

"That's not fair!"

"Take it or leave it."

He took it.

"You eat too many sweets, see!" Vanessa mocked him.

"Don't nag your brother, Vanessa," Helen said, and Vanessa stopped. If it was possible to stop something eagerly, that was how she stopped. Helen reminded herself that she mustn't play favorites. As they stopped to look in a shop window, with Vanessa gripping her hand tightly, she laid the other arm across Roddy's shoulders. He shrugged automatically but didn't dislodge it. During this time, Laurent sat in the Citroën, wishing he were in South America, and Berry lounged in a doorway, very careful to keep out of sight. There were perhaps twenty people in the little street and a regular string of through traffic. This was not the place. From his doorway, Berry approved of Helen in slacks. She was not the kind he would like to be seen around with, but for what he had in mind, she was fine. He wouldn't have to force himself from a sense of obligation. When she and the children finally got into the little car, he went back to the Citroën with a swagger and a thin little smile. Laurent looked at him in undiluted terror.

Helen found a small beach. There were two other families on it, but this she didn't mind at all. Her strong sense of reticence didn't include nervousness about appearing in a bathing costume, as Berry imagined. Such an idea would have struck her as neurotic, and she had prizes from a score of swimming galas besides. She briskly dismissed any suggestions of sitting down to eat at once.

"We all eat too much," she told the children. "Anyway, you don't go on a picnic to guzzle, you go to *do* things. You're both going to learn to swim today."

"I'll sink!"

"You'll come up again."

Roddy was apathetically pulling off his shoes and trying not to look as if he was looking at Helen unbuttoning her blouse. She tried to remember how early boys developed a prurient interest in sex. Surely ten was too young? No, of course it wasn't, a class of ten-year-olds was always flickering with whispers and undertones. A dangerous age. She grinned at herself and threw the blouse into the car. The system was to be brisk and matter-of-fact, and she hauled her slacks off in the most matter-of-fact way she could manage.

"Do you like my bathing suit, Roddy?"

He shot an unwilling glance at her, then turned away and mumbled. Helen laughed.

"You're not very flattering!"

"It's all right, I suppose. Who's interested in bathing suits?"

"It's lovely!" Vanessa gazed in adoration.

"So is yours." Helen ruffled her hair.

"It's not bad," Roddy conceded. "I thought you would look older."

"This is what older people look like." Helen wasn't sure if that sounded right, but at least he was looking straight at her as she rammed her hair into her cap.

"You look all right," he said, almost resentfully.

"I can dive, too."

This time he didn't contradict her.

Berry was sorry he hadn't brought a pair of field glasses, the better to gloat on his prey. He had found a comfortable spot at the top of one of the gentle cliffs that ran down to the water, and the group down on the beach was perfectly plain, but it was far enough away for recognition to be impossible, and he would have enjoyed an unsuspected close-up view of the shy English bit who didn't know what was coming to her. At the far side of the beach, there was a rough road running down to the sand, and the red Mini was parked there. When the time came, he wouldn't even have to short across the ignition—she couldn't have the ignition key in her swim suit.

Laurent was thinking the same thing. He had begun to see the possibility of a quiet snatch which was so simple that even Berry surely must accept it as a gift and give up his plans for revenge on the English miss, who after all had done nobody any harm. The more he inspected the situation, the more Laurent's self-confidence returned.

"*That's* the way we want it," he said and tried to sound positive and forceful. "They go into the sea, we walk down and drive the car away. In an hour, we'll be on the road to Paris and nobody'll ever know anything."

"Let's just take it easy, old man," Berry said. Berry was purring. He was still sorry he didn't have a telescope, but he was purring.

"There's no hurry. I'll get the stuff and my fun as well." He demonstrated his cold resolution and his muscle by snapping a match clean in two with one hand.

"Forget about the bloody woman!" Laurent broke out. "You'll screw the whole thing up."

"I'll forget nothing." Berry had stopped purring. Laurent tried to swallow his nervousness but couldn't. "Are you scared?" Berry demanded.

"I'm not scared!" Laurent was sorry as soon as he had uttered the words. In the first place, they sounded like a lie. In the second place, in a curious way they committed him to accepting Berry's lead. If he had said bluntly that he was scared and that he intended to get the car and to hell with the girl, Berry wouldn't have had an answer. But it was too late. Laurent groped for a way of recanting but failed to find one. He rubbed his hand over his face and settled to wait. It was worse than his years in the coal mine, worse than crouching before a safe in a midnight office. He wasn't only in a hole; he was in the hands of a dangerous lunatic. He lay back and closed his eyes and tried to go to sleep. Instead of sleeping, he merely found himself totting up all his reasons for hating Berry. He felt an affinity with the unsuspecting English miss. He had no grudge against her, and he didn't want to harm her. He was sure she had no grudge against him. He almost felt he quite liked her, in fact. It would be nice if he could be rich and honest and go swimming with her down there instead of sitting up here with a homicidal satyr. Life was lousy.

"This time we'll have no slip-ups," Berry cooed to himself.

"Oh, you're in for an educational afternoon, little English miss."

"For Christ's sake, jag it in," Laurent groaned. With a reckless expenditure of virility, Berry snapped another match and picked his teeth with one of the pieces.

Curiously enough, it was Vanessa who kept sinking. Helen began to wonder if perhaps the little girl actually had a higher specific gravity than sea water. The trouble was that Vanessa had so much passionate confidence in Helen's instruction that she eagerly lifted her feet off the bottom and threw herself blindly on the buoyancy of the water, and each time she went down like a stone. Roddy, darkly suspicious of the salt water, gingerly lifted his feet and then scrambled like a drowning man. He got sick of this carrying-on very quickly, but he was so insulted when Helen broke off to demonstrate a few slick crawl strokes that he launched himself out face first again. He was even more insulted when a small French girl sliced past him with her face totally immersed.

At the twentieth patient attempt, Vanessa gave a wild cry. "I'm swimming!" Then she vanished beneath the waves. Helen yanked her up, and the pale little face spouted water in all directions and coughed. "I did it!"

"I think you've had enough for the day, Vanessa," Helen told her, and the little girl became passionate and stubborn.

"No, no! Just watch!" She threw herself at the water and performed three distinct strokes.

"Anybody could swim like *that*." Absolutely disgusted, Roddy mimicked her frenzied thrashing and disappeared. He came up exploding.

"I swum. Hey, I swum!"

"Why shouldn't you?" Helen demanded.

89

"I thought it took weeks." He glowered at having been deceived. "It's a cinch."

It was delicious to swim in sea water that was actually warm. A far cry from rushing in, cringing, to the bleak embrace of Brodick Bay in that gray north country. Helen jack-knifed lazily and slid along under the surface and came up to terrified screams from both children, who were sure she had drowned.

"You get octopuses in the water here!" Roddy complained, in an attempt to sound manly and brutal like his father. His lips trembled. Helen raced them up the beach to start on the picnic supplies.

Berry didn't mind how long they took. Delay improved the chances that the other people on the beach would go away, and there would be no need for haste while the trio were still in bathing suits. He was gratified to see first one and then the other family gather up towels and gear and leave the beach. Helen hardly noticed their going.

"They're going for a walk," he told Laurent.

"Yeah."

"The kids are coming up this way."

"Uhuh."

He could hear the English miss shouting instructions after them while she tidied things into the car, and he had a start of apprehension when he saw her putting on her slacks. But she couldn't drive away without the kids. No, it was all right; she was coming after them. The little girl was in the lead, in a climb straight up the hill toward Berry and Laurent. Quite some distance behind, the English miss was scrambling after them.

"It's worked out great," he told Laurent, who looked drearily over the hill and watched the children without saying anything. In a few minutes the little girl reached the top, and was taken aback to see the two men. The little boy came after her and glowered at Berry and Laurent.

"Allez-vous en," Berry snarled.

"Leave the kids alone," Laurent told him.

"Let's go back, Roddy," Vanessa said.

"I'm not going back! We'll climb the next one. I can beat you." He circled Berry warily, and Vanessa circled behind him. Berry made a jerking movement toward the children with his hand, and Roddy started back and then ran, with Vanessa panting at his side. He stopped a few yards away and shouted back, "You're a stinking French pig! Yeh, pig!" Vanessa tugged at his hand.

"You do what you like," Laurent said quickly. "I'm going round to get the car."

"You leave the car alone!" Berry's voice was rasping and violent. "We get the car together."

"I'm having nothing to do with this anyway."

"Who asked you?"

Disgusted, mostly at himself, Laurent got up and walked away in the direction the children had taken. He was barely out of sight when Helen scrambled, panting and laughing, over the edge of the plateau. She went on laughing for a few moments after coming face to face with Berry. Then she stood and panted. Keep walking past him, don't stop whatever you do, her mind insisted. Panting more heavily, she put her best foot forward.

8 *ROSEMARY KNEW WHAT ALBERT WANTED TO*
do. He wanted to bury himself in some pub and booze the
afternoon away, cracking dirty jokes with men or, worse still,
eyeing French teen-agers in bikinis. She had no intention of
allowing him. It was the first time they had got rid of the
kids for a whole afternoon, and she was looking forward to an
orgy of shopping, with Albert in tow, looking as fed-up as he
liked, but carrying parcels the way men did in . . . in car-
toons? That was how married men went on shopping orgies.

Albert was quite willing to admit that Rosemary was dead
right. He did want to bury himself in some pub. He had had
enough sunshine for one day, and he didn't fancy trailing
round shops in Saint-Tombe either. Being nobody's fool, Albert knew he would end up buried in some pub; in a particular pub, in fact. He could either tell Rosemary to go to hell,
or he could play it crafty. He played it crafty. For a start
he told her, women didn't want men around when they were
messing about in shops, and for another thing, he loathed
shops. Having said this, he obediently joined Rosemary and
then kept on saying it. It didn't require much subtlety to
sneer at everything she fancied in the shop windows and insist
on walking fast past the windows Rosemary wanted to see.

"They got nothing but bleedin' beach junk," he said. "The

prices are daylight robbery as well. Come on, I'm sick of standing here."

In half an hour, Rosemary told him to go and drown himself in booze for all she cared, and she was sincerely glad to get rid of him. He agreed to meet her in the bar of the Canaris in two hours, and apart from threatening to kill him if he was drunk by then, Rosemary didn't complain. Albert went rapidly to the bar of the Canaris and sat at a corner table with a Campari and a lot of soda. A nice kind of drink that would keep you sober if you had to spend a long time alone.

This time, at last, Sevink arrived. Albert had spent only fifteen minutes in the corner, and was wondering if the little dark piece at the bar was likely to be worth trying, when Sevink came in out of the sunlight, looked slowly round the room, and then came over to sit beside him.

"May I join you?"

"Yes, sure, sure. Have a drink. Hey, waiter! Garçon!"

"You are very kind." A bit of a frog, old Sevink—not a French-type frog, a real frog. His eyes seemed twice as big as normal people's, and they had an awful lot of lid, and his lips kept laying themselves flat together so that they stuck out in front. Like a frog's.

"On holiday here, then?" That was a bloody silly question, Albert knew, but if Sevink wanted to play it cunning, O.K., so would he.

"I rent a house outside the village. I may even buy it. Property is a burden to a free soul, but I find this free soul is best adapted to encumbrances."

"That kind of encumbrances, sure," Albert agreed fervently.

"One can be poor in comfort only if one has money," Sevink said.

"Bags of money, sure."

"You know the works of Oscar Wilde?"

"Who? Oh, him. He was a bit of a queer, wasn't he?"

Sevink pushed out his lips to indicate civilized distaste.

"Your most beautiful stylist. I greatly admire his development of the paradox."

"Oh? Can't say I've had much time for that. I believe he was pretty good, mind you." If Sevink wanted to talk about everything else under the sun, that was jake with Albert, who prided himself he could keep his end up in any conversation. To his relief, Sevink abandoned Oscar Wilde and started to inquire politely about the family and the holiday. Albert began to enjoy the talk, and was able to offer some shrewd comments on the French way of life and climatic differences. They had several Camparis.

It was almost a shock when Sevink suddenly asked Albert if that was his car outside.

"That? Yeah, sure. It's a beauty, showroom condition—only 1,500 on the clock—" He suddenly remembered he wasn't trying to sell it. "Yeah, why?"

"Well, naturally I have an interest in your car, Mr. Moore." Albert stared at him, wondering if there was a catch somewhere.

"Oh, that!" he finally caught on. "No, no, that's not the car. It's my sister-in-law's car you want. That's the one with the . . . you know, the little something extra?"

Sevink was not pleased.

"Where is it?"

"It's O.K., don't you worry, Mr. Sevink."

"I am not in the habit of worrying, Mr. Moore. Worry is too good for the health. Um, worry is too soothing to the nerves. . . . Mr. Moore, where is the car?"

"Well, it's like this, my sister-in-law took the kids on a picnic with it, you've got nothing to worry about."

"I should like to examine it without delay, Mr. Moore. I find cars too interesting, they're so unmechanical."

"What do you mean?"

"No, that wasn't up to Wildean standard, I admit it willingly. I wish to have the car examined tonight."

"Nothing to it, I'll bring it along."

"Your sister-in-law won't object?"

"No, why should she? Well, actually, she is a bit fussy about it—you know what women are. Don't worry, I can talk her round."

"That shouldn't be necessary, Mr. Moore. Bring her to my house for dinner. Will she come?"

"Yeah, sure, that's a very very good idea. Oh. I don't know if my wife would like it."

"Ah, wives do have an urge to husband everything."

"Ha! That's a good one!"

Sevink was modestly pleased.

"Do, I beg of you, bring your charming wife too, Mr. Moore. I am most impatient to meet . . . all the components of your family."

"Don't I know it!" Albert felt easier now that Sevink was happy. "You've been watching the car close enough anyway."

"What do you mean?"

"Oh, come off it, I'm not a mug. Some of your boys have been hanging round the house, haven't they?"

"I don't have boys, Mr. Moore. And none of my employees would hang anywhere without my orders. What are you talking about?"

"Ah, it's nothing, I suppose." Albert tried to persuade himself that it was nothing. "You know what spinsters are, my sister-in-law had some cock-and-bull story that somebody was hanging about the yard last night. You know what I mean, she's never had a man, you know how it gets them sometimes, they see men everywhere."

"I very much hope you're right, Mr. Moore. I very much hope you haven't developed any ideas about—changing the plan, for instance?"

"Me? Look, all I'm doing is acting as a bloody errand boy, I don't want to get mixed up in anything else."

The two men looked at each other for a few seconds, Sevink sallow and cold and remote, and Albert first angry, then defensive, then sullen.

"And your sister-in-law is away with the car—to some obscure place—this afternoon, you said?" Sevink pressed his lips together so firmly that they almost curled outward, like these darkie blokes with soup plates in their face, Albert thought. Albert shrugged, felt a bead of sweat above his eye and started to think back on what exactly it had been that Helen had said about having something thrown over her head.

"Have another Campari," he said. His voice came out falsetto.

"Well, mademoiselle?" Berry smiled engagingly at Helen.

"I'm in a hurry." It was a muttered gasp. She was still breathless from the climb, and her chin trembled with surprise.

"No hurry." Berry stepped lazily in front of her.

"Get out of my way," she said impatiently. He gripped her arm and threw her down on the grass with a force that drove the remaining breath from her lungs. She stared at him with popping eyes, and her mind beat and struggled to free itself from terror. Berry took a knife from his pocket and the blade snapped into view. Insane, she thought, and then thought: the children. There must be a way of protecting the children, from . . . whatever it is.

"Get up," he said. She shook her head weakly. Berry laughed and kneeled beside her.

"Get up, mademoiselle."

She put a hand on her heaving chest and shook her head again, trying to indicate that she didn't have the strength. He must be placated. Perhaps he didn't intend to murder her. If not, he could do anything else as long as the children weren't involved. Berry laughed, and ran a light finger over her bare shoulder.

"How nice to meet you again, mademoiselle. You've been avoiding me," he added roguishly. Helen fought the sick weakness of her body and panted fervently to get oxygen into her bloodstream. She wouldn't panic—whatever happened she would think clearly. Berry smiled at the frantic heaving of her chest.

"You're frightened. That's good." The light finger trailed down to her waist, and she nodded, with her eyes fixed on his. If he liked her to be afraid, she would be afraid; she would be even more afraid than she was, if that was possible. Her tortured lungs were beginning to settle, but she kept on panting. He held the knife close to the side of her face.

"Get up."

She stood up. Berry stood close to her, and the knife was even closer.

"What do you want?"

"You."

"I have two children . . ." It wasn't difficult to sound frantic, to impersonate the truth.

"I don't want them," Berry smiled suavely. Abruptly he grasped the waistband of her slacks at the front and pulled her against him.

"Monsieur, I beg you . . ." In spite of herself, she shuddered violently, and Berry smiled again.

"A little kiss, mademoiselle." He bent his face toward her, and she held her face up, unresisting. His lips pushed against hers in a contact without meaning. Berry found himself irritated. He pushed her away and jerked his hand back, still gripping the slacks. They gave way at the zip and he let go. Instinctively Helen grabbed to keep them from falling. Berry smacked her hard on the right cheek.

"Please, monsieur!" She hung her head as tears started into her eyes, but now there was no question of panic. The slap had been a mistake. She merely detested this vicious stranger, and as she moved her head to blink the tears away she was scanning the grass for a stone. A stone, a log of wood, anything at all. The time had come to plan. Berry's hand was under her chin, and he forced her head up.

"A little pain, a little love. I'll teach you the lesson, mademoiselle." She stood with her eyes closed.

"Why don't you struggle, mademoiselle? Why don't you scream? I don't mind."

"The children. . . ."

"Ah, the children mustn't know." She felt one of his hands grasping her and kneading her hip. "Put your arms round me, mademoiselle, be affectionate."

"My . . . my clothes. They'll fall down," she said lamely.

"That's right."

She put her arms round his neck, but her feet were spread apart. She wasn't worried about the humiliation of her slacks falling down, it was the thought that they would trip her up that concerned her; Confucius, he say, man cannot run with trousers down . . . woman neither, she thought. Berry ran a wet tongue across her lips. It was nauseating. She had seen a stone, a beautiful stone, about eight inches long and four across. He pulled away from her and began to drag down one of the straps of her swim suit, and automatically her hand came up to stop him.

"We must be quiet for the children, mademoiselle." He grinned. The stone was too far away. She could never get to it. She forced herself to smile, and he slid the strap further down her arm. I wonder if he knows how damned hard it is to drag off a wet bathing suit, she thought. Berry was thinking the same thing. This was not going to be difficult, however. He put the knife back in his pocket and took the other strap in his right hand. Helen wriggled, smiling, and obligingly lifted her right arm out of the clinging strap and jabbed two fingers murderously into his eyes.

For an instant she was going to stop and put her arm back in the strap, and she almost wept at her stupidity. But she was already four yards away, and she had the stone in both hands. She had, she realized, absolutely no idea what she was going to do with it. A blow on the nape of the neck—would that produce insensibility? It wouldn't do him any good, at least. But she had no time to select a method. Blinking but not quite blind, Berry had located her, and he was rushing at her with hands grabbing. She threw herself between his arms, holding the stone before her and swinging it downward. She didn't hear any sound as it struck his face, but her

99

left thumb leaped in agony. Berry stopped and his hands waved upward toward his face, and Helen stopped, paralyzed and fascinated.

The children, the children. They were probably miles ahead by this time, and it would take hours to round them up, and he would still be here, more murderous than ever. She found that she still had the stone in her hands, and she considered smashing it into his face again. He swayed, with his hands over his face, and a trickle of blood running down between two of his fingers. She couldn't bring herself to strike him again. Her one concern now, and it was desperate, was for the children. She ran to the edge of the hill and almost fainted with relief when she saw them tracking across the beach toward the car. They must have climbed down and come round by the water.

Berry was still standing, like a very drunk man, holding his face. She held her waistband in one hand and started to scramble recklessly down the slope. A gun, a gun, perhaps he had a gun. But there was no question of dodging; she was already moving so erratically that it would have been superfluous.

When she got to the car she knew that she must say nothing. The important thing was to get the kids aboard and get away.

"I couldn't follow you." She tried to laugh. "My zip came unstuck. Come on, it's time we started for home."

To her surprise, the children hopped into the car without a quibble. She sat at the wheel for a second or two, licking her lips and rubbing her palms on her knees to dry them. Then she pressed the starter, and let out a long sigh of pleasure as the motor kicked instantly. She took the rough road up from the beach with great caution, in first gear, to avoid any possibility of stalling or slipping.

"Aunt Helen!" Vanessa shouted. "A man swore at us in French."

"I called him a stinking French pig," said Roddy.

"That was very naughty of you, Roddy." The reproof came unthinkingly.

"There were two of them at the top of the cliff," Roddy said doggedly. "They had a big black car."

Helen's wrists tingled. Of course they would have a car. They might run her off the road—children and all. Two men? Probably it was two different men altogether. But any man on these cliffs would have a car. She pressed her foot hard down, and Vanessa yelled with triumph.

"Seventy-five!"

"Are you sure it's safe?" Roddy asked, gripping his seat hard.

A big black car. These French cars were terribly fast, Helen seemed to remember. And there was something implacable about them, somehow. She held the wheel tightly and crouched over it.

Berry found Laurent splashing sea water into his face, without gentleness. Finally he let Laurent pull his hands away so that the water could reach his features more easily.

"She hasn't ruined your beauty," Laurent remarked, with a tinge of regret.

"The bitch, she'll suffer for this." Berry's voice was a little thick and quiet. His head ached horribly. He had not been knocked insensible, but his skull was still ringing from the impact of the stone on his forehead, and blood was coming from a line above one eye.

"She stuck her fingers in my eyes," he said, in wonderment. "Treacherous bitch. She was so frightened, I thought. By God, she'll be frightened next time."

"What next time?" Laurent asked.

"We can catch her now!" Berry shouted. "Come on!"

"We could have taken the car an hour ago," Laurent said thoughtfully. "You know that? We were both sitting here, the car was there, everybody was swimming. We could have had the car an hour ago, and we could have been on the way to Paris now. Rich."

"All right, all right. Let's get the car now!" Berry shook himself and wiped his eyes.

"That wasn't good enough for you," Laurent said dreamily. "You want to screw somebody as well, to prove you're a big boy. You bloody useless infant."

Berry put his face close to Laurent's. He had already gauged the little coal miner's strength, and he was in no mood for a turning worm in his present condition of pain and rage.

"Just mind your tongue, old man," he said. "Just mind it, boy." With a gesture of weariness and disgust, Laurent swung his forearm in a chopping movement into Berry's mouth. More outraged than hurt, Berry put his hand in his pocket. Laurent gripped him by the biceps and tightened his fingers until Berry shrieked. Laurent reached into the young man's pocket, took out the knife and threw it over his shoulder. Then he released his hold and struck Berry again in the face. The young man reeled backwards, whimpering.

Helen realized she couldn't keep up a steady seventy-five miles an hour. It was too great a strain on the nerves. She felt Roddy sigh with relief when she slacked off to sixty.

"Roddy did something else too," Vanessa suddenly burst out, and Roddy muttered, "You shut up."

"Well, you did!"

"Don't clype, Vanessa." It was too much to have to listen

to a squabble as well. "What did you do, Roddy?"

"Well, they asked for it!" Roddy blustered.

"What did you do?"

"He let down the tires of their car! That's what he did. He did! You did too, so don't deny it."

Helen began to laugh.

"Oh Roddy," she gasped. "Je t'adore!"

"What's that froggy talk?"

"It means I love you. And I love you too, Vanessa," she added quickly.

"Un deux trois," they chanted. "Quatre cinq six!"

9 *BY THE TIME SHE REACHED THE HOUSE,*
Helen had come to what seemed to her a simple and reasonable decision. She would leave France next day, or as soon as
she could get space on an air ferry, and tour Cornwall instead.
It was ridiculous, certainly, after all the time she had spent
dreaming of a French holiday, and it was sad, when she loved
the scene and the sunshine and the atmosphere of Frenchness
so much. No doubt other women were accosted by men and
dismissed the experience, even if it was really ugly. No doubt
women were accosted by men even in Cornwall. But in spite
of her arguments with herself, she couldn't throw off the cer-
tainty that she had been singled out, individually, by name,
for this persecution. Like a fatalist in wartime, she thought,
who believes that the bomb with your name on it will get you
regardless. Well, fatalism was fine, but if you actually identi-
fied the bomb with your name on it, the only rational proce-
dure was to move to a place where the bomb wasn't.

What saddened her most of all was the suspicion that if
she turned her back on France now, if she ended her visit
and retreated, she might never come back. From long habit
of examining herself clinically, she recognized that for the
rest of her life her impression of France—perhaps her impression of all foreign travel—would consist of two days in which

she was inexorably pursued by a sex maniac with a switch-blade. And why her, of all people? Nevertheless, she was resolved to leave the country. Abroad was wonderful, but no matter how well you spoke the language, there was something homely and comforting about Britain, where you knew how everything worked and where you understood the police, even understood the criminals if you did meet any.

She had also decided to say nothing to Albert or Rosemary. Or to the police, if France's police were represented by that nincompoop Jumeau. If she was a hysterical spinster, she would keep her hysteria to herself, stand on a woman's normal right to be changeable and simply go.

Albert and Rosemary were at home when she drew up outside the little courtyard. She let the children scramble out of the car and fill the silence with shrill recitations of how they had learned to swim like fish. One blessing about children was that they created an endless earsplitting diversion and averted embarrassed silences. She was able to go into the house and change and wash, and restore her composure. She congratulated herself that she couldn't be too hysterical when she stood on the cool tiled floor of her little bedroom and peeled off her bathing suit, still damp in patches. Of all costumes, this was the most wildly inconvenient for a rapist. Sex maniacs must be crazy as well as insane. She shuddered and scrubbed her lips to remove the memory of Berry's wet tongue. She couldn't throw off a sensation of being trapped, of being at the mercy of an ugly force in a foreign land. The feeling would persist until she was aboard a plane for home. But she had no intention of living in panic until then. Without saying anything to Albert and Rosemary, she would make sure that she was never away from them until she left for Le Touquet. When that time came, she would drive with both care and speed, and it shouldn't be too difficult to keep close to other cars all the way on that busy route, comfortably in sight of other, respectable citizens.

She dressed in a white flowered cotton with a shoulder strap top and a full skirt and got the routine ogle from Albert when she joined the family in the courtyard. They were having tea in the open air. When the breathless tales of the children had worn down a little, Albert began to explain that she was invited out to dinner, and her first reaction was to refuse, to cling to the house and refuse to move.

"You want to get out and enjoy yourself," he insisted. "Anyway, I promised."

"Are we all going?"

"No, just the three of us, the kids can stay with Marie, it's all fixed," Albert said.

"I don't care what you promised," Rosemary said, "I'm not going. I've got a headache."

"Oh Christ, you and your headaches!"

"I've really got one this time. It was those drinks, so early in the day."

"What do you mean, you've really got one?" Albert demanded angrily. "You mean it's an alibi all the other times?"

"Please don't shout, my head's splitting." Rosemary was quiet and cold and martyred.

"All right, then," said Helen. This affectionate scene was all she needed to confirm her in her decision to get away. Two weeks of married bliss with Albert and Rosemary suddenly seemed too much for any visitor. "You go, Albert, and I'll stay in with Rosemary."

"Fine. Jake with me. I don't give a damn. I'll have a damn

sight better time on my own!" Albert lunged into the house to find cigarettes, rapidly calculating that a small adjustment would put the Vauxhall out of commission for the day and that he would be forced to borrow Helen's Mini without the inconvenience of having Helen included.

Rosemary was pleased at having won the battle, but she immediately began to suspect her triumph when she realized how willingly Albert had surrendered. She did have a headache this time. She also had about four hundred francs' worth of bits and pieces she had bought during the afternoon, and the most soothing program she could think of for the evening was to sit quietly and go over them, try on a couple of things and gloat over the others. She also didn't want Albert to go out with Helen and leave her, Rosemary, behind. She didn't trust Albert an inch. But it was hard to tell whether it was worse or better for him to be going out on his own. As likely as not he would try to get off with some French piece. And at least he wouldn't *get* anywhere with Helen—Helen was too frigid to fall for Albert's ideas if he had any.

However she looked at it, she had to make some compromise, and after stroking her forehead sadly for a few seconds, she cast a pale tortured smile at Helen and said, "No, it's not fair, after you've been stuck with the kids all day, Helen. You go out with Albert, you'll probably quite enjoy it. It's this man he met, quite rich, I believe. French."

Helen thought very quickly and decided that Albert would be more reassuring company for the evening than Rosemary. With all his faults, he was big and beefy. She shrugged her agreement.

"Well, what have you finally decided?" Albert asked surlily, and Rosemary gave him a sweet, wan smile.

107

"You and Helen can go. I'll stay at home with the kids. I'll feel better resting, honestly," she added, to make everybody feel happy.

"Anything you say," Albert conceded. "Will you drive, Helen? There's a funny noise in my engine—tappets, I think. Overheated." He didn't trouble to invent a feasible engine trouble. Helen wouldn't know the difference between a tappet and a boot lid.

At this moment Paul Pennard put his head in the courtyard gate and then advanced diffidently toward them. Albert gave him a scowl. Albert had reacquired all his suspicions of every stranger since his conversation that day with Sevink. This slimy little Frenchie could be up to any God's thing. Helen rose and went quickly to Pennard. He was the only adult in Saint-Tombe who gave her any feeling of confidence and assurance, and she found herself responding to his appearance with pleasure and relief.

"For God's sake, get rid of him," Albert muttered. "Give these people an inch and they take a mile. Can he not see we're having a meal?"

Helen walked through the gate to the street outside, and Pennard followed her.

"It's a pleasure to see you again, monsieur," she said.

"You are too kind, mademoiselle." Perhaps her greeting had been too flowery. She had intended only to be pleasant and polite.

Pennard looked at the little car thoughtfully and then started to speak just as Helen began to frame a casual remark. They apologized to each other, friendly, embarrassed.

"No, please continue, monsieur."

"I'm sorry, mademoiselle, I may not be able to do this little job for you for a few more days."

108

"Oh. It doesn't matter, really."

"My . . . my young brother-in-law had an accident on one of the scooters."

"The young man—the young man who—oh, I am sorry, monsieur."

Pennard shrugged.

"It's not too serious. Concussion. A few bruises. Still, he's in bed for a few days. It makes it a little awkward to leave the garage. If you don't mind, mademoiselle."

"No, of course not, your family is more important than this scratch."

"You're very kind, mademoiselle." This was unnecessary, Pennard himself felt. But he liked Helen. Anyway, it was true, she was kind—one could tell these things. And probably she didn't get many compliments. They smiled at each other.

"In two or three days, I will do it. I promise, mademoiselle."

"Oh." Helen smiled again and pursed her lips, in the mannerism she was trying to cure—the schoolmarmish pursing of the lips.

"Please don't worry about it, monsieur. I'm leaving for home tomorrow, I think."

"Ah! So soon! And the weather's so beautiful."

"Well, you understand, affairs."

"Ah, it's a pity, all the same."

In spite of her resolution, Helen had to tell somebody. "This holiday is not lucky for me, I'm afraid." Pennard looked at her quizzically, and she changed her mind. "Ah, it doesn't matter, you have your own troubles, monsieur."

He shrugged those away. She had fine shoulders, darkened by contrast with the white cotton. The little lines at the corners of her mouth pleased him. Yes, she was kind, he thought. But firm too, fine good steel inside: a quality he hadn't found in many women except his mother-in-law, who was a different proposition, after all. He smiled at the thought.

"You're worried about this . . . this man who followed you," he said.

"Yes, frankly, I am. I met him again." She had now decided not to tell him. It was too ugly, and there was no point in it. But Pennard waited, clearly expecting more. She waved the subject away.

"What does it matter?" But she shuddered.

"What does he look like?"

Helen laughed. "You have your own troubles—you shouldn't waste your time listening to a hysterical spinster."

"I enjoy it. I like the way you speak French."

They laughed, and Helen found herself looking straight into his eyes. She looked away, casually.

"Oh, he's tall, about . . ." Five feet ten? Seventy, divide by two, multiply by five, "One meter, seventy-five. Oh, there's the point o four. It's very difficult, monsieur."

"Quite tall, then."

"Yes, very handsome, yellow hair, blue eyes, young, about twenty-six."

"Mm! One would recognize such a man."

"One hopes not to meet such a man, monsieur. Anyway," she became brisk again. This jolly chitchat with a married man wasn't good enough. "Anyway, I am leaving for home tomorrow."

"Is he still here?" Albert was at the gate. "What the hell are you nattering about?"

"I'm just going, monsieur," Pennard said, in very reasonable English.

"Hurry up about it, then."

"Would you mind not interfering, Albert?" Helen felt a flush creeping up her cheeks.

"Take your hands off that car!" Albert glared at Pennard, who had turned away to avoid Helen's embarrassment and was stroking the scratched fender lightly.

"Mind your own business, Albert!"

Albert had already lunged forward and taken Pennard by the arm.

"Just leave that car alone, mate. I won't tell you again!"

Helen was stunned with fury. Pennard, looking profoundly embarrassed, straightened up and twisted, and Albert fell back suddenly, clenching and unclenching his hand and glaring at the Frenchman.

"I'm extremely sorry, Monsieur Pennard," Helen said wildly, and he offered her a half-smile.

"I should not be the cause of a family quarrel, mademoiselle. Good-bye, and a good trip."

"Yes, you'd better clear off," Albert muttered, as Pennard turned and walked away.

Helen turned and glared at Albert, bottling her fury in the hope of finding a phrase that would shivel him properly. Finally she said, between her teeth, "You can go out by yourself tonight, Albert. And I'm leaving tomorrow."

"Now don't be like that, Helen! It just gripes me when these damned foreigners start snooping round—there's too many funny characters around this place. I know, I know, it's none of my business. Helen, I'm only thinking about you, for God's sake. Aw, come on, Helen, don't get me in the doghouse, Rosemary's bad enough already." He tried to put his arm round her in brotherly love, but she pushed it away.

"All right, all right," she conceded. "Don't go on about it." They walked into the courtyard to find that Rosemary had gone indoors to nurse her headache and unwrap some of her shopping.

Paul Pennard walked the few hundred yards to his home and visited Charles' bedroom. Madame Robet was sitting by the bed, not touching her son but staring fixedly at his pale unconscious face. Moved to pity, Pennard patted her shoulder, and she clasped his hand.

"He'll be all right, maman," Pennard said quietly. "Go and occupy yourself with something, I'll watch him for a while."

"Oh!" Madame Robet grimaced at her own motherly weakness. "He'll be all right, all right. Fools are lucky." She pressed Paul's hand and flounced out of the room to fret in privacy. Paul stood looking down at the bed, shaking his head. The unconscious boy stirred, and Paul sat down beside him. The eyes remained closed, but Charles moved uneasily under the sheets, and a vapid smile appeared on his face.

"You don't know," he murmured. Paul watched him without speaking. "You don't know . . . I got the stuff . . . none of your business . . . I know . . . I never touched any car . . ." The dreamlike mutterings sounded characteristic of Charles, big secrets, vague boastings that meant nothing. Paul stared at him, in pity and exasperation. Charles slept.

A few minutes later Madame Robet crept upstairs to tell him that there was a client in the yard, and Paul went down.

"He wants to hire a scooter," Madame Robet whispered.

There was a young man in the yard, looking over the scooters with a decisive eye.

"I wouldn't like to depend on any of these piles of junk," he said.

"They're not very flashy," Paul agreed. "They work."

"So you say."

There was someting familiar and unlikable about the young

112

man, who stood in the long shaft of sunlight in the courtyard. Instinctively, Paul stayed in the shadow and kept his head down. Even without the description, he knew the man for the hitchhiker he had met in Le Touquet, the one who had been molesting the English miss.

"Do you want one?" He tried to keep his voice husky and coughed so that he could bow his head and put his hand in front of his mouth. "Ten francs a day."

"Bloody robbery."

"Take it or leave it."

"Ten francs for twenty-four hours?"

"That's it. Fifty deposit. The red one's best, it's full up."

"Better than nothing." Berry pulled the money from his pocket and held it out. Paul summoned up a paroxysm of coughing and took the money crouching forward.

"Anything to sign?" Berry asked.

"No, nothing." Paul's only object was to get rid of him, get him out of sight. Berry shrugged and went over to the red scooter, which he kicked experimentally all round before he settled to starting it. Evidently he was familiar with scooters. Paul retreated to the doorway of the house and waved before he turned inside. The motor coughed and then roared, and in a second or two the machine was putting out of the garage yard. Paul leaped from the doorway and grabbed an old push bike. He pedaled out into the street, glanced right and saw, as he expected, that the red scooter was heading in that direction. It wasn't traveling very fast. Paul followed it without haste on the bicycle.

Berry traveled only a few hundred yards before he turned the scooter off the road into a piece of vacant ground. Paul wheeled into the roadside, leaned against a wall and waited. He saw Berry coming back onto the road, cross to a site where a new villa was being built and sit on the ground under the shade of a half wall. He was in a convenient place to keep an eye on the house where the little red Mini-Minor stood outside the courtyard. Pennard sat on his bicycle, leaning against the wall and whistling soundlessly for several minutes. No one came from the house. The blond young man lit a cigarette and relaxed. Paul lifted his bicycle round and pedaled back to the garage. It was none of his business if hysterical spinsters had men following them—he noticed he himself had fallen for the phrase "hysterical spinster." Hysterical? Whatever that one was, she wasn't hysterical. She was a formidably rational English miss. No, Scots miss, he remembered. Even more rational, then. And there was nothing hysterical about the blond young man who had hired the scooter. He was real, and if Paul was any judge, he was a nasty bit of work. True, the Scots miss had protection in that bulky brother-in-law, but it was a flabby kind of protection. Anyway, Paul told himself, why not admit it? You fancy the dame, a bit.

"Is that you, Paul?" Madame Robet called. She came to the doorway. "I thought you had gone out."

"Just for a minute, maman. I'm going out again, though. As long as you don't mind, that is."

"Why should I mind?" She bridled.

"Oh, you know, with the kid in bed. I don't want to leave you if you're worried."

"No, no, Paul. Paul!"

"Eh?"

"Oh, nothing. It was kind of you to ask."

"Tripe."

Madame Robet stood uncertainly in the doorway and then went inside. Paul kneeled beside the blue scooter and started

114

to take out the plug. A fresh one would do no harm. On an impulse, instead of straightening up, he stayed squatting on his heels and did a Russian dance from the scooter to the shed with the old plug in his hand.

Berry sat in the shade of the half-built wall, quite soft and relaxed, rationing his cigarettes. He could wait all night, if necessary. It was better to work alone, with no share-out, of diamonds or anything else. He was sorry he hadn't killed Laurent for daring to strike him, but he might catch up with Laurent later. He had left the little coal-miner doggedly blowing up the tires of the Citroën to drive back to Paris like the yellow little rat he was. Laurent didn't have the mind or the temperament for a real job. He was better out of the way.

In the courtyard of the little house, Roddy and Vanessa were campaigning to screw a promise from Albert that he would swim with them tomorrow. Albert was warning them how expert a swimmer he was and trying to find a way out of backing up his boasts. Upstairs, Rosemary was unwrapping what seemed to Helen an entire warehouse stock of small parcels for her admiration. Musical boxes, cigarette lighters, underwear, perfume.

"You must have spent a fortune." Helen couldn't prevent herself from saying it.

"But it's not as if I was spending it on myself," Rosemary answered virtuously. "You have to take *something* back to your friends."

"Yes, of course. Well, that means an economical trip for me, I haven't got that many friends."

"Oh, for heaven's sake, Helen, there must be a few of the old neighbors in Stirling."

"I, eh, I don't even know if I'll go back to Stirling."

"What do you mean?" Rosemary was startled, shocked, even. "Holidays are all very well, but you've got to go back home sometime."

"Home? I don't really have a home," Helen said calmly.

"Oh, I know, Helen, it must seem lonely now that father's dead. But it's still your home."

"Mm." Helen dropped the subject so obviously that Rosemary became nettled.

"Well, it is your home. I mean, you've got your job and everything, even if it is a bit lonely just now."

"Just a minute, Rosemary." Helen couldn't see how it concerned her sister, but in a family, you always had to be explaining yourself. "It isn't lonely now that father's dead. O.K., I was sorry to lose him, but living as a spinster daughter with a crabbit old man was never my idea of a great time. Now I'm on my own, I can go anywhere I like. I think I'm due for a wee change. A teacher can get a job anywhere."

"You talk as if father had been an old dragon," Rosemary said, hovering on the brink of tears. "He was . . . well, he wasn't."

"You didn't live with him." Now why can't I simply say, "You took damned good care you wouldn't be stuck with him"?

"Well, naturally, I was *married*."

"Yes, I'm not complaining."

"I don't know what you would complain about."

Helen smiled, then burst into laughter. Rosemary stared at her, defying her to speak, but Helen shook her head and picked up a musical box to admire it, and the moment passed. It was impossible to be brutal to Rosemary, and in any case, it served no purpose. The past was past. What would it serve to recall old days, when Helen was being half wooed by an ambitious young car salesman, and Rosemary suddenly up and married him? Rosemary had Albert, and Helen's romance would probably have petered out of its own volition in any case. It was interesting, certainly, that Rosemary's abrupt capture of Albert had occurred just when their mother's illness had begun to look like the final illness, when the house was going to consist of a crotchety widower and two marriageable daughters and somebody was going to have to take care of father. Somebody had always taken care of father. Twelve years of youth were down the drain, but twelve years with Albert might have been worse. Would have been worse.

"Anyway," Rosemary was saying, "you've got the house. You can't leave that."

"I'm selling it."

"You've got no right to sell the house!"

"Why not?" Helen was bland. "It's mine."

"Yes, I know it's yours, legally, but I mean, it's the family home."

"Look, Rosemary. You have a house, and I have a house. If you want to sell yours, it's O.K. with me. If I want to sell mine, it's O.K. with me too."

"Father wouldn't have wanted you to sell it, Helen. I don't think it's right."

"No doubt. Father wouldn't have seen the sense of anybody in the world going on living after he was dead. But I'm selling it."

"You won't get what it's worth." Rosemary was bewildered and disoriented by the news, and Helen felt she understood why. Helen, in Rosemary's eyes, was the sister who had missed the boat and who would always be there, safe and convenient. It was against nature for Helen to move away, to abdicate her responsibilities, even when the responsibilities were ended.

"I've been offered two and a half thousand," Helen said, almost sorry for delivering this terrible blow. Rosemary was utterly dumbfounded.

"Father couldn't have known that," she babbled.

"Probably not. I like this perfume."

Rosemary's jaw dropped and she stared at the wall of the bedroom. A dozen protests whirled through her mind, but none of them could be uttered without sounding wrong. She had been her father's favorite daughter—she had always known that. Father hadn't even minded her going off to get married so soon after mother's death. She could never do any wrong in father's eyes. And he had left her everything in his will— everything except the house, that is. A tidy thousand pounds in cash among other things. She had felt quite sorry for Helen, after all those years, getting nothing but the dark old house that Rosemary had been so glad to escape from. It couldn't have cost more than seven hundred pounds when father bought it, long before the war. Father couldn't have known it would be worth so much now. Even Albert hadn't mentioned the possibility, and Albert always knew about the price of things.

"There's a boom in property," Helen said gently.

"Oh, I'm not saying you're not entitled to it, Helen, heaven knows you're entitled to anything after staying with father all those years. It just doesn't seem . . ."

"Never mind, Rosemary—you've got Albert." Helen was aghast at her own malice, but she kept her face solemn and gentle. "And the children. A spinster does need some consolation, even if it was an accident."

"Yes, you're right, Helen. Oh, why am I bothering about

the rotten old house? You deserve every penny. And you're quite right, you should get away and . . . do whatever you want."

"Do you really mean that?"

"Yes, I mean it! I'm not *completely* selfish, Helen. I don't know how you stuck it all these years." Rosemary took a tight grip on herself and laughed. "I must admit I'm a bit jealous. Money in the bank and nobody to bother about."

"You would hate it, Rosemary."

"I suppose you're right. I was cut out for the little house-wife. And damned brats. Honestly, they just get on my nerves sometimes. Just you don't let Albert start making any passes at you tonight, that's all."

Helen laughed aloud.

"You're worried? You've got him tied hand and feet."

"Well. I just mean . . ." Rosemary waggled her head, be-trayed by a complacent smile. The sisters laughed at each other, and Rosemary threw her arms around Helen's neck. Nothing was changed, but the past that Helen had always avoided so carefully was genuinely past.

Berry stood up and stretched and strolled along the street to the little café for a glass of cider, leaving the red scooter standing on the vacant ground. He drank the cider without wasting time and strolled back to his seat in the shade of the half wall. He paid no attention to the three men at a table— the postman, the butcher and a mechanic in overalls who kept his head bowed over his glass all the time Berry was in the bar; or to the blue scooter standing round the side of the café.

10

FROM THE WAY ALBERT TALKED ABOUT HIS
new friend Monsieur Sevink, Helen could have expected anything. She had never bought a second-hand car, but she
divined that Albert must sound like this when he was selling
one—a mixture of jocular deprecation and enthusiastic sin-
cerity. Sevink was a great bloke, she would love him, edu-
cated, very good family, one of those old French families. Not
that that meant anything, he was quite an ordinary customer,
she might even find him a bit dull, but he was all right, very
friendly, he meant well—pretty witty, you know, sophisticated,
they could look forward to a real French dinner with all the
trimmings. Oh, something simple, maybe, you know what
French people are like at home, nothing fancy.

Helen endured this for a mile or more, with the curious
feeling that Albert was talking to conceal some nervousness.

"How well do you know this Sevink, Albert?" she asked
finally.

"Oh, a bit—I don't really know him, exactly, I just met him
in that cocktail bar. You'll like him, though."

"Have you ever been to his house?"

"No, not to his house."

"Well, how do you know what kind of dinner he'll give us?"

"Well, you know what I mean."

"No."

"It should be good enough, he's loaded."

"Albert, you sound as if you were getting ready to put some big deal over."

"What do you mean by that?"

Helen laughed aloud.

"Albert, you're *always* putting over some big deal. Are you selling him a car?"

"Oh. Well, you never know, a guy like that, there's always a chance. Is that a pair of white pillars?"

"Yes."

"Right first time."

Albert swung the little car—he had insisted on driving—through a gateway and up a steep drive. It was already dark, but an electric light burning outside the house showed up an old stone villa with a slightly pompous portico, and another light shone over a new and unsuitable car port containing a vast American car. Albert threw the Mini-Minor into the space beside it, with an unfeeling ease which Helen deeply envied. A side door of the house opened at once, and a muscular man in a dark suit came out.

"Good evening, sir, good evening, madame," he said, in thickly accented English, and this was evidently the limit of his English, for he waved a hand to usher them back to the front of the house. The garden beyond, in the fringes of the light, appeared to be drenched in monstrous hydrangeas. A portly, middle-aged man was standing on the portico before the open door, holding out both arms in welcome. Like a bishop embracing his flock, Helen thought. He was dressed in a black silk suit with an impossibly white shirt and an almost white gray silk tie.

"Welcome, most welcome," he said. He shook Albert solemnly by the hand and took Helen's arm to lead her indoors.

"Solitude is a blessing," he said, "when one has friends to share it."

"Oscar Wilde?" Helen asked. Sevink's hand tightened on her arm.

"My dear, another devotee! Ah, the paradox. My own, I fear, and a humble thing."

"Not at all. Very convincing." Helen decided he was a harmless nut, but her heart sank at the prospect of an entire evening with any kind of nut.

"Oh, Helen's very up on the literary stuff," Albert was saying.

"Alors! We shall have an evening of the most delightful. Your charming wife is not with you?"

"No, headache, you know."

"Ah, a great pity. But then, perpetual good health makes one so unwell, don't you think? Now you must have something to drink."

The room into which he had led them was long and high, and it should have been graceful except that the furniture was heavy and ugly. Only the generous electric light prevented it from being downright gloomy. Helen cautioned herself against making generalizations about the French home, but she found it strange that Sevink, with pretensions to some kind of literary taste, should live in such a glum house. She found herself holding a very large dry Martini that tasted like neat gin and sipped it with apprehension. Albert had already almost drained his glass, and his face instantly registered the effect like litmus paper. At once, as if a safety catch had been released, he began to talk. Sevink listened with quiet politeness and nodded appreciatively to a rambling monologue about the Common Market and the car industry.

"For myself," he told Helen during a brief interval, "I

favor a United States of Europe. Only when we remove all frontiers will nations be able to misunderstand one another properly."

Oh my God, she thought, how did I get here? She smiled brightly to show that she had caught the joke, which Albert was trying to work out with a slow doubtful nodding of the head.

Albert, however, had a salesman's capacity for accepting any situation. Helen found boredom pressing in on her as he and Sevink exchanged meaningless conversation, and Sevink smiled incessantly, with his soft, straight lips pressed together till they protruded quite half an inch from his face. Oh well. She took a couple of solid gulps of her Martini and decided to enjoy the evening somehow.

"What is your business, Monsieur Sevink?" she asked. That's what all the magazines said—ask a man what he does and the conversation will never flag. Sevink and Albert looked quickly at each other, a reaction that registered faintly on Helen, and then Sevink smiled again.

"Business is my business, my dear," he said. "I am not interested in commodities, simply in moving them from one person to another. That is what I like about business—it is so unbusinesslike." Even Sevink didn't think he had scored a hit with this one, because she could see him trying to think of a fresh way of phrasing it. She wandered idly to the window at the end of the room and looked out into dead blackness, which she realized must be steeply falling ground down to the sea.

"You have the water at your doorstep, Monsieur Sevink. How fortunate."

"Ah, yes, but I try not to get my feet wet." Sevink laughed, and so did Albert. Helen joined in dutifully.

"My man will serve dinner in a moment," he went on. "Let

123

me fill your glass again, Miss McLeish. A full glass looks less abstemious."

At this moment the door opened and a man came in; not the same one who had appeared earlier. This one was thinner. Sevink turned to him, smiling, inquiring.

"Quelqu'un dans le jardin," the man muttered.

"Par exemple. Trouve-le," said Sevink. "Sans bruit, hein? Et surtout, gardez la voiture. Presse-toi."

The man nodded and vanished. Sevink turned to them and smiled.

"Forgive me. My man says all will be ready in ten minutes."

"Is that what he said?" Helen asked the question casually.

"Yes, he is just finishing the table now."

"Why did you tell him to watch the car?" Helen looked straight at Sevink and smiled.

"You are mistaken, mademoiselle."

"Who is in the garden?"

"I don't understand, mademoiselle." Sevink pressed his lips together. He looked so bland that Helen had an impulse to slap him.

"Forget about the car, you're here to enjoy yourself," Albert said. There was a note of anxiety in his voice that alerted Helen at once. "She's nuts about that car," Albert explained to Sevink. Albert was sweating.

"I feel rather warm," Helen said quickly. "I think I would like a breath of fresh air."

"Finish your drink first, mademoiselle." Sevink's smile was wearing thin. She twirled the glass in her fingers.

"Just stay where you are, Helen, and don't go poking your nose—"

"There is something very funny going on," said Helen. She put the glass down and went to the door. It was like a dream, only slightly removed from reality. She saw Albert lunging toward her, his face red and angry. She opened the door and ran along the hall to the front door, which was lying open. There are too many damned odd things going on, she thought. This is the limit. It was the word "voiture" that had quickened her senses, she realized. Her little car seemed to have a curse on it, and she was flying to protect it with the maternal fury of a tigress. Albert shouted after her. She swerved to the right to make for the car port, which was now in darkness. She tripped and landed messily in a giant hydrangea bush. As she lay, her eyes began to distinguish shapes in the dark. The car port was still to her right, farther away than she would have expected, perhaps twenty yards. A small light flickered inside it—an electric torch, perhaps.

Suddenly the main light flashed on. A man crouching over her small red car straightened up. There was no logic but some kind of inevitability in her recognition of him. It was the blond young sex maniac hitchhiker. He twisted suddenly as the light came on and stood with his back to the little car. The burly manservant shot out of the side door of the house, launching himself straight for the hitchhiker, who smashed his electric torch into the man's face. It didn't stop the impetus of his attack. Helen struggled to her feet, kicking flowers aside, as the two men grappled and then fell apart. The hitchhiker fell back, and Helen saw that he was now holding a knife. The manservant poised, wary. There was an abrupt movement in the darkness of the garden, somewhere to her left, and a dark figure rushed into the car port—the other manservant, the thin one.

He landed in the hitchhiker's back, striking downward with his hands, and both men pitched forward. Now the burly servant joined them. Helen's hands went to her mouth. The three men were thrashing about indistinguishably on the concrete beside the red car. One of them rose with his back to her—the thin manservant. He had the knife in his hand. Now the hitchhiker heaved himself upright. He was brightly lit by the overhead bulb as he lunged forward to meet the thin man. They locked, and the thin man stepped back.

The hitchhiker stared straight out into the darkness of the garden, straight into Helen's eyes. His face was slack and his mouth hanging open. He stood, staring, and Helen stared back, hypnotized, for two, three, four seconds. His hands were crossed over his stomach. He fell forward to meet his shadow on the white concrete. She could feel the shock of his fall ringing in the back of her head, with a pain that made her eyes swim. She too was falling forward. Over a cliff, into black water.

She had fallen face down, but she was lying on her back. The fact made her suspicious, and she lay perfectly still. There was some coarse surface against her fingers, and she pressed it gently. Not earth, but a rough fabric. Light was striking painfully on her eyelids.

"Are you all right, Helen?" A hand lifted her hand, a hand patted her wrist. Stubbornly she kept her eyes shut.

"For God's sake, Helen, are you all right?" Somebody was always nagging you when you wanted peace. She opened her eyes. Albert's face hung above her, in shadow, wet with sweat but deathly white. He smiled a sick smile.

"Sure, you're all right . . . you . . . ha ha . . . you tripped and knocked yourself out. I don't know what got into you."

"There was nobody in the garden, was there?"

"No, nobody at all! Where did you get that idea? I think the heat's got you." He gripped her hand tightly, and she could feel the trembling of his hand like an electric shock.

126

"Most unfortunate." Sevink's voice came from some distance away. Albert turned his head and said, "Too true. I think I'd better get Helen home. You look terrible, Helen. I'd better get you home. I'd better get you home right away. You want to get home right away, don't you? You'll be all right when you're home."

"We'll wait till Miss McLeish feels stronger," Sevink's voice said.

"No, no, she should be in her bed, at home, that's the game, just get up and get her home. Isn't that right, Helen?"

"O.K." Helen tried to return the pressure of his hand, to stop him trembling.

"We all need time to relax." Sevink's voice came from somewhere behind her head, like a psychiatrist's. "To tidy up. You understand? Miss McLeish will need time to *tidy up.*"

"Oh. Yes, tidy up. Yes, we can't go home without tidying up, that's right, you're right, old boy. Don't worry, Helen, as soon as we're tidied up I'll take you home. I could use a drink." He got up and picked up a glass from somewhere. Helen turned and saw him leaning heavily with one hand on the table, holding the glass to his mouth with shaking fingers. Sevink swam into her range of vision.

"Such an unhappy ending to our little evening, Miss McLeish," he said kindly. "You tripped on the doorstep, remember?"

"Yes, I must have got my feet wet," she said foolishly. She felt cold. She was lying on a sofa in the lounge where they had been drinking. The door opened and the thin manservant came in, and Sevink turned to greet him. The man had a small black object in his hands, a box or a piece of black stone. Sevink took it from him and laid it on the table. Sevink too was pale. Albert, still leaning heavily, craned over to

127

see Sevink as Sevink held the black thing and broke it into two. Then Sevink looked up at Albert. Albert stared at Sevink's hands. They stood like this, interminably: Albert, white and gaping, Sevink pale and still, the manservant behind Sevink, quiet and poised. When Sevink spoke, his voice was husky and tortured.

"What have you done, Mr. Moore?"

The tableau remained frozen. Albert licked his lips and gaped.

"What have you *done*, Mr. Moore?"

The manservant moved a few steps farther into the room.

"Answer, Mr. Moore!"

"Christ, it's got nothing to do with me!"

Sevink dropped the two black pieces and put his hands to his brow, rested his fingers lightly on his temples.

"Where are they?"

"I need a drink." Albert tottered to the sideboard, to fill his glass and drain it. Sevink remained standing at the table, with fingertips pressed to temples.

"I wish to know, Mr. Moore," he said finally, lowering his hands and smiling. "Knowledge makes one so agreeably ignorant." Albert stared at the table and waved his arm in despair.

"I don't know a bloody thing about it! I never even saw them. This is your pigeon, Sevink, don't think you can start blaming me. I don't want anything to do with it."

Sevink stared at him in unbelief.

"You don't want anything to *do* with it, Mr. Moore! You already have everything to do with it. Va-t'en, Savaron," he muttered to the manservant, who stared at him and unwillingly left the room.

"Now," said Sevink, "we shall sit down and have a friendly conversation. Sit down, Mr. Moore. Sit down!"

Albert stared sullenly at Sevink and then sat slowly in a chair by the table. Sevink pressed his hands flat together in front of him and rocked back and forth on his heels.

"We shall have a friendly little conversation and elucidate our problems, Mr. Moore, before you go home."

Helen swung her legs off the sofa and pressed herself upright.

"Albert and I are going home, Monsieur Sevink," she said levelly. She stood up, dizzy.

"You will sit down, Miss McLeish."

"Albert and I are going home, Monsieur Sevink. Now."

Sevink walked to the sideboard, opened a drawer and turned round with a pistol in his hand.

"If you try to leave the house, I shall shoot you dead, Miss McLeish," he said.

"No you won't." Helen walked carefully toward the door. "Come on, Albert." Sevink laughed and put the gun in his jacket pocket.

"You're quite right, Miss McLeish, I won't shoot you dead. I shall do nothing, and your brother-in-law will be guillotined."

"You're crazy."

"Hey, what the hell are you talking about?" Albert's voice came in a shriek. Sevink turned to him, not smiling.

"There's a dead man not far from here, Mr. Moore. I can disappear without trace. You don't know my real name. Can you disappear without trace?"

"Nobody can disappear without trace." Helen's voice insisted on betraying her uncertainty. Black horror swept over her.

"There was somebody in the garden," she said dully. Sevink ignored her. Albert buried his head in his hands and started to weep. The spectacle exasperated Helen and brought her to her senses.

"Albert!" she said sharply. "Albert!" It was like getting through to a sullen schoolboy who has already denied his guilt to himself. "What is this all about? Albert!"

Albert continued to weep into his hands.

"It's quite simple, Miss McLeish," Sevink said. Helen watched him carefully. His little mannerism of pressing his lips together had not deserted him, but now he was doing it about twice a second. A smooth, precious, frightened man. "Mr. Moore undertook to deliver a small consignment of goods from England. Quite a valuable consignment. He has not delivered it."

"It's a damned lie!" Albert looked up desperately. "Now don't you start pinning anything on me, Sevink, I know nothing about it. All I did was lend your chum a car for the afternoon. It's none of my business what he did with it."

Sevink's glance was thick with contempt.

"For a thousand pounds, it is very much your business, Mr. Moore." Helen stared at Albert with a different kind of horror.

"It was my car, Albert!" He returned her stare, denying all blame.

"That does seem mysterious, I admit," Sevink said, looking at Albert.

"God, don't start going all holy on me!" Albert yelled at Helen. "O.K., it was a bit of smuggling, is that so bad?"

"But you used my car!" The sense of betrayal was unbearable.

"Well, who's the best bet for fooling the Customs? Somebody innocent! Anybody knows that! If I had brought them I might have given the game away. You can't beat a clear conscience." The slogan popped up automatically from twenty years of selling dud cars.

"And what was it I was smuggling?" Helen was trembling with anger.

"How the hell do I know? All I did was lend them your car for the afternoon."

"I think he knows, Miss McLeish. It was diamonds. To be exact, sixty-three uncut diamonds."

"Stolen."

Sevink shrugged. Business. Helen's anger began to concentrate itself on him, and she sat down and remained very still. The knowledge that Albert had used her, had exposed her, perhaps to imprisonment, she filed away in the hope of forgetting it. It was too appalling to think about. Once she had expected that she might marry him. She was lucky, in an odd way. But loathing Albert could achieve nothing. He too was a mindless pawn in the game. This womanish, smooth-faced, pouting Sevink was the source of villainy, and it was Sevink who had to be defeated. She concentrated on his face, to exercise a violent mental image of Albert kneeling under a guillotine. Did they still use the guillotine in France? In any case, the idea was quite irrational. No matter what Sevink said, he couldn't disappear and leave Albert to be arrested for murder. It didn't fit. For the moment, she had not analyzed her own danger, except the danger to her that might come from Sevink. She took a deep breath and tried to organize her thinking.

"You've been hijacked," she said. Sevink looked at her in puzzlement.

"Somebody else has stolen the diamonds from you."

"I have never had the diamonds!" Sevink shouted.

"I was attacked the first night I arrived here," Helen said, through her teeth. "Somebody knew they were in my car."

"Who?"

"The same man who followed me from Le Touquet—the blond young man. . . . "

"A man who has stolen something doesn't take the trouble to try to steal it a second time." But before he spoke she had already realized the truth of this. And that was the explanation of her persecution. The hitchhiker wanted the diamonds. Wanting her was merely a bonus. She shuddered, for she had just again seen his slack face falling toward her in the darkness of the garden.

Sevink sat down in an ugly armchair and gave every appearance of relaxing. The silence stretched until Helen almost giggled. Not even Sevink knew what to say next.

"Well," she said finally, and the word clanged in the room, "I'm very sorry about your diamonds, but we can't help you, so Albert and I will have to go home."

"Don't be foolish, Miss McLeish. Nobody is going home until I get my property."

Albert turned his blotched face to Helen, with hard, dogged thinking visible on it.

"Did *you* take them out?" he demanded. Helen gave him a look of such disgust that he started to shout. "Well, you had a better chance than me! I never even touched them! I never saw them!" He turned wildly to Sevink. "Maybe she's got them in her luggage!"

Sevink turned slowly to stare at her, and she sat quietly, seized with an instinct that it was clever to say nothing, to be one up on Sevink, to keep him wondering. She could feel Sevink's eyes fixed on her.

"Let's go home and look," she said finally. Anywhere outside would be better than being trapped in this house. Sevink shook his head without even considering the suggestion.

"All right, I'll go and look!" Albert offered. Sevink shook his head again.

"You are safe as long as you are here, Mr. Moore."

"Don't be a bigger fool than you look," Helen told him crisply. "Albert can't tell anybody anything. He's up to the neck in this as well. And if he doesn't go home tonight, Rosemary will call the police."

"By God, that's right, she will!" Albert clutched at the suggestion. "I told her I would be early."

Watching him, Helen wondered if he could be relied on. If he had half a brain, he must know that he had no connection with the killing in the car port. If he had half a brain, he would get straight to the police and have her rescued. If he had half a brain. The trouble was that he did have half a brain, but he was in such a condition of funk that he was unlikely to use it. She could imagine him getting out of the house and fleeing blindly in any direction.

Sevink was sitting back with his eyes half closed.

"Yes," he said finally. "You will go home, and look through Miss McLeish's luggage, Mr. Moore. Miss McLeish will stay here. I am beginning to think she may know something about my property after all. In any case, one of you is staying here." He smiled coyly. "If Miss McLeish does not come home early, you can explain that she found my company too interesting to leave. And you will remember she is here, Mr. Moore!"

"Yeah, sure, sure. Don't worry." Albert got up and pulled himself together. A degree of cheerfulness was breaking through. Helen had never despised him so much. But he was a husband and father, and he was needed more than she was. She turned sourly from this pretense of heroism. If she had been able to think of another suggestion, she would have fled and left him instead. He turned at the lounge door, and over Sevink's head, framed the words "Where are they?" with his lips. Helen looked at him blankly.

"Oh God," he said.

Sevink stood at the open door and shouted to his servants. Helen sat on the sofa, heard the sound of the engine starting, and then the to-and-fro of gears as the car reversed onto the drive and moved away. Sevink sat down again and stared at her. The psychological treatment, Helen stared at him.

"This must look very silly," she said.

"Shut up!" He was not happy at all, but the discovery didn't please her. If he was baffled and desperate, he might behave stupidly, and he had a gun. The lounge door opened, and the thin servant came in. Servant? His shoes were wet, water splashed from them onto the polished floor.

"We'd better get rid of it and scram!" he said urgently.

"Shut up!"

"What do you mean, shut up?"

"I want my property!"

"Ah, stuff your property. Give us a hand to get the stiff in the boat, or you can spend your property in hell."

Sevink turned on him in a fury.

"You do as you're told! I want my property!"

"Listen, buster!" At least, it sounded like the French for buster. The thin man wasn't behaving like a servant any more. "You can either give us a hand or we'll scram and leave you here—and the stiff. You explain it."

"What about her?" Sevink's lips were flapping.

"That's your business. Knock her off as well."

"My brother-in-law knows I'm here," Helen said quickly.

"Merde!"

As the thin man said this, his knees buckled under him and he shot forward on his face, with another man on his back, a man in overalls whose clasped hands rose and fell on the thin man's neck.

"Monsieur!" Helen screamed. Paul Pennard scrambled to his feet. A shot sounded with deafening volume. Sevink was standing by his chair, with his pistol pointing in the air. He lowered it and pointed it at Pennard.

"Damn and blast," Pennard said, "I thought he was outside." He made a gesture expressive of idiocy.

"Stand back against the wall, both, please," Sevink said, and shouted, "Jean! Jean!" Jean was already at the door, wild-eyed at the sound of the shot. "See to Savaron," Sevink said, keeping the gun pointed at arm's length at Pennard.

"What a bloody mess," said Jean. He kneeled beside Savaron and started to slap his face from side to side.

"Not at all, not at all," Sevink smiled again. "Let us avoid panic." Savaron was coming round dopily. "The operation has been unfortunate, but there will be others. Perhaps we had better get rid of these two as well."

"For God's sake," said Jean, "do you know how far it is to the boat?"

"If you kill me, you'll never see your diamonds, Monsieur Sevink." Helen kept her voice steady.

"Damn the diamonds," said Jean. "Come and get rid of that . . . luggage." Sevink was staring at Helen with his eyes narrow and his lips pushed out again.

"We can lock them in the cellar while we finish the urgent work," he said. "Then, with our consciences clear, we may find the property. I know, I know, you need help. Kindly move to the door, mademoiselle and friend."

Jean stepped aside to let them pass, eyeing Pennard warily and hefting a cosh. They were ushered to a door at the rear of the hall and Sevink ordered them through. Helen followed Pennard onto a tiny landing and down a flight of wooden steps. Light suddenly appeared, from a naked bulb in the center of the low ceiling.

"We shan't keep you long, mademoiselle and friend," Sevink said, from the doorway. "Do try to remember where my property is, or I shall kill you both." The door slammed, and there was a grating sound of bolts going home. Helen and Pennard stood, staring up at the doorway.

"I saw you being knocked down in the garden, mademoiselle. I should have done something then." He didn't look at her.

"Monsieur Pennard, you are heroic, veritably."

"I am an imbecile."

"Yes, an imbecile too." Her hand reached out timidly to touch his arm. "Why did you do it?"

"Ah, who knows? For the sake of the tourist industry, I suppose. I like tourists." He had begun an inspection tour of the cellar. "Perhaps you will tell me what it is all about?"

"I've only discovered what it's about. It's a long story. I suppose this is a silly time to worry about runs in my stockings."

"To worry about stockings, mademoiselle, is to be a woman, and alive." He looked at her stockings, and she blushed.

"Well, it's a long story."

"Go on talking. I listen well even when I am doing other

136

things." He continued to scan the walls and floor of the cellar.

"I feel better now that you're here," Helen admitted.

"Me, I feel terrible. Therefore keep me entertained with the story."

"It isn't very entertaining, but I'll try."

11

"IT ISN'T POLITE TO CRITICIZE YOUR FAMILY,"
Pennard said, "but your brother-in-law is a bad man."

"He's more weak than bad." Helen's protest was half-hearted.

"He is the weak man who makes evil possible. Now, you can sit on this or lie on it. We may as well rest while we wait." He had dragged old sacks together to make a thin layer on the earth floor, with an almost-clean, dry piece of canvas on top. During this operation, Helen stood idly by, watching. He seemed to need no help. His matter-of-fact movements made the task seem like a routine job he did every day with skill and economy.

"What's the use of resting? There isn't time, is there?"

"Time enough." He was now emptying a packing case onto the floor and rummaging through the old rubbish it contained. "It's a long drop from this house to the shore." He kept on rummaging. "If I wanted to put something in the sea so that it would never be found again, I would take a long time to carry it all the way down. Then I would have to find enough weights to sink . . . the thing. Then there are strong tides on this coast. I would want to go well out to sea before I threw it away. Then I would have to sail my boat back to the same place—it isn't as easy as you might imagine, it takes time to find the place, Then I would have to walk up the cliff again. There is plenty of time to rest. And I don't think any of those three are sailors. An hour on a speedboat's a different thing from the Channel at night. There is time to rest."

"You make everything sound much more hopeful, Monsieur Pennard."

"Ah, hope is easy. We shall give hope some assistance. Ah!" He picked up in triumph a dusty coil of electric flex. "A weapon!" Before Helen could ask how it could be converted into a weapon, he was already climbing the wooden staircase. She followed him and watched in fascination while he found a place to string the flex tightly across the staircase, a foot above the fourth step from the top. He pulled it to test its strength.

"Perhaps yes, perhaps no. Perhaps yes."

"That's marvelous!" Helen was joyous as a child.

"One should never put a prisoner in a cellar, mademoiselle. There are too many useful things in the cellar."

"But they might see it."

"Not with the light out, mademoiselle."

"But the switch is outside the door."

"Ah, mademoiselle." His tone was reproachful.

"Yes, of course, yes, I'm an imbecile. Yes! We take the lamp out!"

"And that is another weapon, mademoiselle."

"I would never have thought of it."

"You would have thought of it if you had been alone. I think you would have thought of it, mademoiselle."

"Thank you."

"So. We are in good luck. We are two, and we can plan, and neither of us is a hysterical spinster."

"Thank you again, monsieur."

He smiled at her, a quick flash of comradeship that warmed her absurdly. For a moment, she was an excited schoolgirl engaged on a delicious practical joke. Much the best way to look at it.

"It is really very foolish of them to imprison us in a cellar, monsieur."

"And why should they not be foolish? They are only petty thieves."

"Not Sevink. He isn't petty. He's queer, but he's really a what-d'ye-call-it. A master criminal. I didn't know there were such people."

"Come come, mademoiselle, this is romance. The only quality common to all criminals is stupidity. A man with a brain can make more money honestly than any criminal ever made. Was a burglar ever a millionaire? Trash."

He was rummaging again through the junk from the packing case, laying every solid object in a neat row on the floor.

"The artillery. Perhaps we'll have no need of it. Can you throw?"

"Yes."

He looked at her from under his brows.

"A good answer, mademoiselle. À nous la victoire."

"No Pasaran."

"Yes, that too."

He was rummaging again. Like a tidy, efficient mole or an intelligent squirrel.

"It's a pity," he said, "our host hadn't left a few bottles of old brandy in his cellar. Not a very civilized man. Still, we can have a cigarette. And rest." He sat down on the pile of sacks, and Helen awkwardly sat beside him. The front of her dress was smeared with dirt from the garden, and her ruined stockings embarrassed her. She wished she could find some easy matter-of-fact way of taking them off.

"It's the first . . . that is to say, I don't often get locked up with a man." She hoped her laugh sounded gay and light, but to make sure, she added quickly, "I hope—I mean, your . . . family will be worried about you."

"Ah." He waved this away with his cigarette. "My family have other things to think about." Busy with his eyes, still calculating the resources of the cellar, he had missed her hesitation. Helen wondered about the wife she had never seen, the wife he dismissed so nonchalantly. Sharp and shrewish, like his mother-in-law, perhaps, or dull and fat. She tried to put the thought out of her mind.

"I am not a child." He grinned. "I'm allowed to stay out late."

"How old are you?" The question came unthinkingly.

"Forty."

"Oh."

Pennard leaned back on one elbow and watched a thin stream of smoke from his lips, completely at ease. The hand holding the cigarette was square and bony, the fingernails square and cut short. One of them was broken . . . Helen let her eyes wander past it and fasten on the brick wall beside the stairs. There was nothing more to say, nothing more to do. She felt a profound embarrassment.

"Good Lord, it's only nine o'clock," she said.

"Mm?"

Sevink was also in the grip of embarrassment, among other things. Cabas and Savaron were doing most of the work of carrying the heavy body down the cliff paths, and he was occupied mostly in shining a torch to light the way for them. But even this was undignified enough. Quite apart from the hideous danger of running into a stranger, or falling over a pair of lovers, he was oppressed by the miserable indignity of it all. It wasn't his line of country at all.

He was a businessman, a high-class buyer and seller. If his business sometimes required violence, the violence was cleanly taken care of by employees in his absence. There had been plenty of routine violence, but nobody had actually been killed before, at least not by his direct responsibility; and never in his presence. It wasn't murder, of course; it was a mere accident of self-defense. Nevertheless, it was enormously regrettable, and dangerous. And undignified. And unprofitable. He wished from the bottom of his heart that it had never happened, and he wished that the next hour was behind him; he wished he was eating a good meal in Nice or Paris or America.

Cabas and Savaron would not consider any implications wider than the immediate danger and the quick disposal of the body. They were simple animals. But Sevink's profession was to think ahead, to think of everything, in a shrewd businessman's way. He could disappear, it would be best to disappear, with or without Cabas and Savaron, probably better without them; they would keep their mouths shut—they had done the killing, after all, not he.

But there was the question of the girl, and Moore—and the little man in the cellar, whoever he was. One mustn't panic. Moore: he was up to the neck in it—he could hardly be blamed for the murder, if it ever came out, but Moore was, Sevink now realized bitterly, a stupid man, or this whole mess would never have developed. And he was a frightened man,

142

and he would *think* he might be guillotined. Therefore he would keep his mouth shut. It had probably been foolish to let Moore go at all, but the alternatives were equally chancy, and there was always the possibility that Moore would find the diamonds in the girl's luggage and be glad to hand them over to get himself clear. Sevink devoted a few seconds' thought to cursing himself for adopting complications, as he had with Moore.

There were a dozen other, straightforward ways in which he could have transferred the diamonds from London to France after paying so dearly for them. He had had to think of a master stroke because the English police were alert for any trace of the biggest jewel robbery in ten years, and he had never been quite sure that he wasn't known in some way to the French police. And it *had* been a master stroke, Sevink assured himself. Not really complicated at all, on the face of it. Find a respectable but corruptible man—Moore had been typecast for the part—and bury the diamonds in a tourist car for collection on arrival. It was only Moore's craven stupidity in using his sister-in-law's car instead of his own that had ruined the operation.

The emergence of the blond young man, at that moment being dumped in the darkness while Cabas and Savaron rested their arms and legs, was a development that baffled Sevink. Moore must have talked to somebody—even he, Sevink, hadn't known that the stuff was in the little red car. Or, and a quiver of alarm went through him, perhaps Cabas had talked.

Cabas! The glaring obviousness of it broke on Sevink like thunder. Cabas. My God, Cabas had done the job on the car, and Cabas had never even mentioned to him that it was a little red car and not a Vauxhall. Cabas must have told somebody else. He swung the torch on to Cabas' face. Cabas blinked and cursed, and Sevink dropped the beam. Perhaps Cabas actually had the diamonds already.

Slowly, now, slowly. No, it wasn't logical. He knew Cabas. If he had the diamonds, he would have vanished without waiting a moment. If the blond young man was his accomplice, why should he be trying to find the jewels when they were already gone?

There was a deeper mystery in it, though Sevink was now positive that Cabas had been in it somewhere. He fervently hoped that Cabas might fall overboard and drown once they were out at sea. An animal and an ingrate. In the meantime, nothing must be said.

All this analysis took only a few seconds, and Sevink was aware how rapidly he had laid out the facts and reached logical conclusions. There was still the question of the girl—it would be ironic if this prim schoolmistress had destroyed everybody by a stroke of luck or cunning; if she had the diamonds hidden amateurishly in a jar of face cream at this very moment. He had a strong desire to shoot the girl dead with the pistol which was in his pocket and which he had never used in his life. But that was an impulse of panic. The girl too was up to the neck in it—she had actually smuggled the diamonds, and she had enough intelligence to realize that she was involved. And she would fear for her fat brother-in-law, the imbecile swine. It was rational to keep the girl in mind. An hour or two locked in a cellar should make her afraid enough to talk. And it would be much more convenient to vanish with the diamonds than without. They represented a debit to date, and debits offended Sevink. It was fifty-fifty that the girl had them. She was worth trying, after she had had time to experience despair in the cellar. If not, too bad. He would have to leave her . . . she could find some way out of the cellar eventually . . . or perhaps lock her in one of the upstairs rooms so that she could escape eventually, when he was well clear. She too would keep her mouth shut.

The little Frenchman, now. He was an unnecessary intrusion. The girl's lover, perhaps. Sevink stumbled over a rock and pain cracked across his shin. Tears sprang into his eyes. He deferred the question of the little Frenchman and kept his eye on Cabas and Savaron. There was another small detail— the awkward kind of detail that could be troublesome. The rent of the villa. He would send the money, with some plausible explanation for leaving early. It was a trivial thing, but an unpaid debt could start people poking around for explanations, as trivial a thing as that.

"I'll take the torch for a bit, you take an end," said Cabas. Ah, the ungrateful villain, Cabas. Sevink didn't argue, but he went on thinking.

Five minutes were endless, and it wasn't really all that comfortable sitting on four or five thicknesses of canvas on top of an earth floor. She had found a position with her knees drawn up, and her skirt drawn down over them to hide her tattered stockings and her hands clasped round her knees. But she was already tiring of the position.

"The most ridiculous thing," she said, "is that you should be dragged into this . . . this situation. It's insane!"

"It's ridiculous that either of us should be in it," said Pennard.

"Yes, I know, but you didn't *have* to be in it. I mean, I'm glad you are—I mean, I'm sorry you are, but I'm glad you're here. I don't understand why, though."

Pennard shifted his shoulders to a new position against the wall.

"I'm a Nosy Parker, I suppose. But why not tell the truth? I was interested in you. One does things for a woman one wouldn't do for a man. It's quite a simple fact."

"That's a beautiful compliment, monsieur." She smiled with difficulty.

"Ah. Who knows why we do anything? We are what we are."

"Tu es philosophe, monsieur. May I say 'tu'?"

"Why not? We are comrades in arms." Pennard grinned to cheer her up and slapped her arm. "Courage, mademoiselle."

"I'll try. Anyway," she said, "I've been thinking. Sevink probably won't come back at all, or if he does, what would he do to us? He can't start shooting us—good heavens, he can't spend the whole night carrying bodies down to the beach and taking them out to sea!"

"No. Maybe not. I don't know."

"Albert will surely go to the police. Somebody will come and get us out."

"Mm. Do you know our police?"

"I've met one of them."

"Ha! Jumeau. There's an imbecile. We have real police, of course. But never depend on anything, mademoiselle. Your brother-in-law is a guilty man. He is worried, that one. I think he might be the kind of man who will wait to see what happens and hope everything will be all right, without taking any risks. Maybe I don't know him well enough, of course."

"No, that sounds like Albert all right." Helen dropped her head on to her knees. "But rationally, we should be all right. I mean, Sevink is a crook, but he isn't insane. What good could it do him to kill us?"

"You're probably right, mademoiselle."

She looked at him quickly.

"But you don't agree."

"One should be prepared for anything. All right, it's true Sevink would be foolish to kill us. But you can't depend on a man behaving intelligently. If he's frightened, he's dangerous."

"Oh God, this is nonsense!" Helen sprang up and started to walk about. "Damn," she said. "Do you mind if I take off my stockings, monsieur?"

"Please do." Pennard turned the other way and lit a fresh cigarette. "Blast the things." Helen muttered, "I can't stand runs. This is absolutely insane." Sick indignation began to boil in her. "I'm just beginning my life, I love it! I've got a million things to do. I'm not ready to give them up."

"You will do them, mademoiselle. Courage, courage."

"Oh, I feel sick thinking about it," Helen admitted. She threw the second stocking viciously away and sat down beside him. "I'm even a virgin."

"That's no crime."

There was a sharp silence, and she blushed. Pennard picked up one of her hands and patted it.

"Stop worrying, mademoiselle, I'm here."

Helen looked into his face, trying to divine quickly all the things he might mean. He put his arm round her and pulled her face on to his shoulder, which smelled of engine oil.

"I only mean," he said, chidingly, "that I'm here, so nobody's going to shoot you." He patted her shoulder, and it comforted her quite ludicrously. She relaxed against him. "Yes, I know," she said. "You're very kind, monsieur. I mean, I wasn't imagining that you meant anything else." She laughed. "Why should you?" she muttered into his shoulder.

"Oh, as for that, I could mean several things, because you're a very attractive woman and I'm a man."

147

She moved back a little and tried to smile.

"You're very kind again, monsieur. I'm sorry to embarrass you."

"Never. What's the time?"

"Twenty past nine."

"Loads of time."

She sat up and stared at the staircase again.

"I've always tried to be honest, monsieur—"

"I believe you."

"—so you won't mind if I say foolish things, since we're in a foolish situation. If I thought Sevink was going to come back and shoot us, if I thought I had only an hour to live, I think I would ask you—"

"Yes, I understand, mademoiselle. But you have a long time to live."

"That's it, I'm not the least bit sure of that. But the funny thing is, I couldn't ask you—I mean, it's the kind of thing that seems logical until it actually happens."

Pennard took her hand again and smiled at her.

"Mademoiselle, it is not logical, not for you. You're not a child, you will not lie with a man out of curiosity. There's more to it than that."

"Oh, I haven't any religious scruples or anything."

"You have your own nature."

Her sense of embarrassment had vanished now that she had finally said the foolish thing. She laughed.

"And you wouldn't be interested."

"Oh, don't deceive yourself, mademoiselle. I am not a nice man, I am a man. But I'm not a child either. You don't do it from curiosity, that would be a waste."

"You are a very nice Frenchman, Monsieur Pennard."

"No doubt. Come, relax."

He leaned back against the wall, and she laid her head on his shoulder without the least awkwardness. His arm rested lightly on her shoulder, her bare shoulder, and she tried to remember how it had felt to have a man's arm on one's bare shoulder ten, twelve years ago. It wasn't the same; she was a different person. She wriggled her head unself-consciously into a more comfortable position, and Pennard's hand patted her lightly again. Her lips brushed his neck, lightly bristled where the razor had missed it, and she murmured, "Sorry," automatically.

"For what?"

"For nothing." She smiled against his neck. He looked down at her, and she looked up.

"You must learn not to apologize," he said.

"Understood."

He twisted his neck awkwardly and kissed her nose, and she wrinkled it.

"Thank you, monsieur." She laughed, a heavy sleepy sound, and as he smiled down at her, the sound stopped in her throat. He touched his lips lightly to hers. They were firm and dry.

"Thank you, mademoiselle," he said. Looking up at him, she heard a faint alarm somewhere in her head. The muscles of her cheeks and her lips were heavy and foolish; her face felt alien and stupid. He kissed her lightly again. It was the bursting of a dam, crazy, impossible; this was not how it happened, it should be a slow growth of pressure, a gentle deliberate thing.

"Bang," she said in English. "In English," she added inanely. "No, no, monsieur, kiss me again."

He touched her lips lightly again and pressed her shoulder to give her comfort. He hadn't realized, he didn't know anything had happened; she recognized the fact dimly and fought to take advantage of it, to control her body into relaxing, to draw back from the edge. As he started to raise his head away from hers, her lips treacherously followed his and his head paused and came down again, still gently, his hand tightened only slightly on her shoulder but she was lost. He drew back and stared into her eyes.

"Oh, monsieur," she said crazily, "my name's Helen."

"Helen. A pretty name." He swung his body and lowered her gently on to the pile of sacks. A pile of sacks, of all things; no, it wouldn't do, it was too ridiculous. He was sitting beside her, and he bent and kissed her, gently again, and her hands had seized him with a greed that made her dizzy. He raised himself slightly.

"My name is Paul."

"Paul, Paul, Paul." His hand rested lightly on her breast, and she felt her skin leaping to meet it. He bent and kissed her on the side of the throat, and she moaned, "No, no, no." He drew away from her at once and smiled down in question. She pulled herself up to him and spoke over his shoulder.

"I'm sorry, Paul, Paul, Paul. The light—I'm sorry, I'm foolish, please be kind, I've never done this before. Not in the light. I'm sorry to be so foolish."

He held her away from him. His smile was so gentle that she felt she would weep.

"Are you sure, mademoiselle? Helen?"

"Oh, yes." She put her fingers to her lips, both lips and fingers trembled. "Are you going to say no?"

"No, I am not going to say no." He kissed her forehead, stood up and lifted the packing case to a position under the light bulb. She saw him flinch as he touched the lamp, draw his fingers back and touch it again, and the darkness was complete. He was still standing on the packing case. She could hear him breathing, hear the sound of his foot as he stepped down.

"A moment, monsieur. Paul. Only a moment, please wait." No, there was one indignity she couldn't bear, although her body felt like heavy oil, powerless and uncontrollable—the long adolescent memory of hands fumbling in clothes, the squalid bathos of garments. He hadn't moved.

"Are you there?" she asked foolishly. A hand touched her hair and found her face. She fell weakly against him in the dark. She pressed his hand to her bare shoulder.

"Monsieur!" she said suddenly. "Paul! You've taken your shoes off!"

"I'm a very polite man." His circling fingers sent shudders through her. "Helen," he said, against her mouth. "Sweet Helen, it may be terrible for you, it may be painful, it may be a terrible disappointment."

"No, no, no, never." Now I'll know, I'll know, I know. I know.

12 SHE HELD HIS HIPS TO SUPPORT HIM AS HE
stood on the packing case and groped for the lamp holder.
She held them familiarly, lower than the waist. They were
miraculous, bone and muscle. Light flooded her and she
blinked.

"I must look terrible." She brushed vaguely at her skirt
with one hand and ran the other hand over her hair.

"I have never seen anything so beautiful, mademoiselle."
He held her hands as he jumped down. Mademoiselle, he had
said. Yes, that was probably the best way. She would have
held him, kissed him gently, still in the impetus of the experience, but this was doubtless yet another thing to learn:
that when it was over, it was over, dismiss it and go on with
other things. And if it ever happened again, it could never
be with Paul . . . with monsieur. Yes, it was best to become
polite again. She tried to imagine living through it again with
another man but couldn't. That's purely an emotional or a
physiological reaction, she decided, the result of an overpowering experience on a totally inexperienced woman. Still, it
was a bleak little thought.

He smiled and patted her on the hip, pretty familiar, after
all. How sweet it must be to be familiar, to live in a state of

familiarity with somebody, two bodies privy to each other as a matter of course. Oh well, to work.

"I feel strangely optimistic, mademoiselle."

"Me too." She smiled, shy and not shy. "To us the victory." He lingered on her briefly. "Sure thing," he said and went to check the wire across the staircase. "Now, mademoiselle, I have had time to do a little more thinking."

"Yes?" She assumed an expression of dutiful attention. The beast. *Thinking. When* had he had time to do a little more thinking? The long-hidden mystery, once revealed, merely displayed further mysteries. As if he had read her mind, he turned and grinned. "I think very quickly, dear mademoiselle." She laughed and shook out her hair.

"What we require," he said, "is an additional element of surprise. Over there, we have a window. It is too small, and it is barred. A mouse might get through it, but we are not mice. Nevertheless."

"Yes, monsieur?"

"Nevertheless. We can create an impression. This is the method. We'll hear the boys coming in, we'll hear the door upstairs. I will then put out the light. You will stand at the window, with . . . with this." He stooped and handed her a tarnished metal dish.

"To break the window?"

"Yes, but not yet. The broken window is of no use to us, what we need is the noise, and we need it after they open the cellar door."

"To get them confused."

"Precisely. You'll see the light from upstairs as soon as they open the cellar door. As soon as you do, smash the window. And stay close to this wall, out of sight, I beg you."

"Just a moment," she said. "What if they just close the door again and run outside to see if we're escaping?"

"Please, mademoiselle. We surprise them. We must hope for some success."

Helen considered the plan. It seemed reasonable, but she tried to put herself in the place of Sevink, opening the cellar door and hearing glass break. Her instant reaction would be to slam the door again from the outside. Pennard could sense her doubt.

"Very well," he said. "Wait till the first one is on the little landing at the top."

"And then what?"

"I demonstrate."

He went back to the staircase and crouched under the little landing at the top, reaching up to hook his fingers over the edge of the landing. Then, with a movement so sudden it startled her, he hurled himself up onto the landing on his stomach and clapped his hands together.

"You see?" He turned his head round to look at her. "I can help him downstairs."

"But you're an athlete, monsieur."

"Please. I'm a little ashamed of it. I hate athletes."

"So do I!" Helen swayed with laughter. "Please keep it a secret."

He shot her an old-fashioned look.

"Very well. That's all we can plan. The only thing is to keep back against the wall. Please do not get shot."

"Right."

Once more there was nothing else to do, and a different quality of embarrassment returned to her. It seemed wrong not to go on loving, but she was feeling her way carefully

154

through a social situation quite new to her, and she was determined not to make any gaffs. This problem too was solved when she sat down on the sacking. He sat down beside her, and then firmly moved her so that she was lying with her head in his lap. He stroked her hair and relaxed, and relaxation came to her.

A long interval passed almost dreamily.

"Paul," she said at last. "Monsieur, I mean."

"Mm?"

"Whatever happens, I want you to know how grateful I am. I thank you."

"You must not thank me for my pleasure," he warned her. "This is not the way to treat a man, unless you know him as you know yourself. It's bad for him. It's I who must thank you. Sweet mademoiselle."

"Thank you, nevertheless. It's a pity it can never happen again. With us two, I mean."

He looked gently at her.

"No. Yes, it's a pity."

A door slammed, and she was on her feet with her heart hammering.

"Courage, Helen!" His hand was on her arm, and he pushed her toward the window. Every muscle was quivering. She picked up the brass plate, and he waved her back impatiently against the wall. He leaped onto the packing case and cursed as the lamp burned his fingers.

Quickly, quickly, she screamed inside.

"Damn!"

The cellar was dark. It was so dark that she realized she couldn't even see the window. Desperate with urgency, she felt along the outside wall and whimpered with relief when her hands slid over the frame and touched glass. She stood with the brass plate only six inches from the pane and tried to stop panting. Footsteps sounded above her head.

Still blinded by the darkness, she strained her eyes in the direction of the staircase, but it was useless.

There was a rasping of bolts and a sudden line of light on the far wall, and before the door was properly open, she heard Sevink.

"Well, my dear, now you know how free one feels in prison!" The line of light expanded to a rectangle that reflected dimly over the whole cellar.

"Miss McLeish!"

Don't rush it, she thought, don't rush it. Now! The brass plate smashed through the glass. The noise was disappointingly small. She crouched back against the wall.

"Miss McLeish!"

Yes, yes, thank God, he was coming down, his feet thudded three times on the wooden stairs before she saw him. He catapulted into her line of vision and shrieked. He fell in a heap at the foot of the stairs, clearly visible in the light from the door, and then nothing happened. There was no movement from Pennard. Nothing. She had the wild notion that somehow he had escaped in the darkness and left her alone. She leaned against the wall and tried to think.

Footsteps clattered again overhead. The shadow of a man fell on the rectangle of light.

"Boss!" The shadow stooped slightly.

"Boss."

A sliding footstep. Watching the shadow, she could tell the man had advanced one pace and no farther, that he was bending to peer down the staircase, cautious and afraid. There was a sudden grunt. Another shadow appeared at the feet of the first shadow. The upright shadow teetered wildly.

"À bas!" Pennard's voice was a heaving grunt. The upright shadow suddenly diminished, and a dark figure tottered downward, threw out both arms and pitched downstairs.

"There's still another!" Pennard gasped. She ran out and saw him scrambling upright on the landing, on the brink of freedom. She had a panic sensation of being trapped in the depths, her way barred by the two men at the bottom of the stairs. They were moving; one of them was getting up. Oh don't panic, don't panic. She stumbled across the shadow and saw that Cabas was getting to his feet, wiping an arm across his face. Even as she registered it, he was beginning to shamble upstairs.

"Look out, Paul!" she screamed in English. Paul had disappeared. Cabas was going upstairs in a stooping position, feeling before him with his hands. To her surprise, she found the brass plate still in her hand. At the fourth step, he discovered the flex, straightened up and stepped over it. She drew back and hurled the plate with all her might.

"Oh, good shot!" she yelled. Of all the idiotic things to yell. It had struck him edge on on the side of the head and knocked him against the wall. But he didn't fall. He put a hand to his head and swayed upward.

The gun, the gun, she thought. That's quick thinking, Helen, the gun, get the gun. *Get the gun.* She threw herself down beside Sevink, who at once began to groan and terrified her. She ran her hands over his body in a frenzy. It was there, there, the pocket was wrong way up, she couldn't find the opening. She found it, rammed her hand inside and started to tug at the gun, which was half under his body. His hand closed over her wrist, and she beat at his face with her left hand, but his grasp was weak in any case. Grunting, she heaved the gun free and fell upstairs. An agonizing pain shot through her knee. For a second she imagined she had shot herself. Then she was up, scrambling up the stairs.

In the hallway, Savaron was clutching his stomach in pain, but Cabas was draped over Paul's shoulders, bearing him down by sheer weight. She stepped out into the light.

"Haut les mains!"

Nobody paid any attention to her. She pointed the pistol at the ceiling and pulled the trigger. Nothing happened. It didn't work.

"Haut les mains!"

Paul had fallen to his knees. She was on the point of weeping with vexation. Safety catches, safety catches! Guns had safety catches! She examined it feverishly, keeping the barrel pointed up and away from her, and wrestled with a tiny lever on one side of it. To her horror, she saw Savaron starting to move forward to where Paul was kneeling with Cabas wrapped round his shoulders.

"Haut les mains!" It came out as a scream, and she pulled the trigger at the same moment. She jumped at the explosion. Savaron started back. At the same moment, Cabas flew over Paul's shoulders and smashed into Savaron. Both men fell violently.

Paul turned to her with a tortured smile, and then his eyes opened wide.

"Throw me the gun, the gun, quick!" She had no time to think. She threw the gun, and he swung right round on one heel as he caught it. There were two podgy hands on her arms, and Sevink was breathing down her neck. She wrestled to free herself.

"Put the gun down!" Sevink croaked behind her. "Put the gun down or I'll kill her."

Paul shoved the gun in his pocket, leaped forward, and grabbed one of Sevink's hands. Helen was thrown against a wall as Sevink yelped and crashed to the floor. Paul had her roughly by the arm and was shoving her along the hallway. Cabas and Savaron were half upright, staring at the gun in his hand. Sevink was on all fours.

"If you go to the police, she's in for it too!" he shouted.

"We'll think about it. Don't move." He swung Helen brusquely behind him and backed toward the front door. "Don't come outside for half an hour. I'll still be out there!" He backed out onto the portico, leaving the door open.

Sevink remained on his hands and knees. He felt mortally tired and wanted to weep.

"Well?" He glared at Cabas. "Get after them, damn you!"

Cabas leaned against the wall and started to light a cigarette. A flat-faced ape, Cabas, a dull ape with something stupid and intractable about him.

"With my bare hands?" he asked without interest. Savaron moved to the doorway and looked out cautiously into the garden.

"The man's standing out there," he reported, "with the gun."

"He won't use it!" Sevink heard the bleating note in his own voice. "You could rush him."

"I don't see the girl," Savaron went on, as if Sevink hadn't spoken. "Maybe she's gone for the cops."

Sevink heaved himself upright and gasped with pain. Think, think, it was essential to think, to isolate his brain from the painful shuddering of his body. But his brain kept shuddering too. Cops cops cops cops cops, it said. Cops. Take it slowly, calmly. He pressed his hands to his face.

159

"She's gone for the diamonds, not the cops . . . Why should she go for the . . . for the police? She . . . has . . . the . . , diamonds. Is that clear?"

Cabas looked at him with his flat ape face, his stupid, stubborn expressionless face.

"How do we know?" The problem didn't seem to interest him. "So we don't know. So maybe somebody else has got them. So maybe she's gone for the cops."

Somewhere at the bottom of his mind, Sevink twitched with a faint quiet sense of alarm. There was something he couldn't put his finger on, some unconscious conviction of danger and betrayal. He stared at Cabas, and he discovered that he was afraid of Cabas.

"Do you know how much these diamonds are worth?" he asked. Cabas shrugged. "We can afford it."

"*We* can afford it? *We*?" Sevink's lips started to shake.

"They might find the body," Cabas said thoughtfully, and Sevink grew really afraid of him.

"That doesn't concern me! I didn't . . . I had nothing to do with it!"

"Oh?" This was Savaron, turning from the doorway to stare coldly at Sevink, and Sevink found that he was no longer thinking about the diamonds. There was no room in his mind for anything but fear. He sat down, slowly, on the floor and closed his eyes.

"The man's away," said Savaron. There was the sudden bark of an engine nearby. It roared and dwindled into the distance. Cabas straightened up.

"Me too," he said. "I'm away too." Sevink didn't look up.

Helen sat on the pillion of the scooter with her arms tight round Pennard's waist. The wind tore through her hair.

"Did you let the tires right down?" he shouted.

"Only two of them!" she bellowed close to his ear. He nodded. "It's enough."

They traveled perhaps a mile, and then he swerved slowly off the road and stopped on the grass. The headlamp went out.

"Something wrong?"

"No. There's another of my scooters back there. We'll have to wait." For the first time, she felt that he had become tense. They got off the scooter, and she watched him strolling back and forth on the grass without saying a word. From time to time a car passed going west. Then he came to her and drew her back from the road.

"This looks like them!" They stood together and looked back toward the villa, where two piercing headlamp beams were rising and dipping on the road. A few seconds later an immensely long, low car whizzed past.

"An Impala," he said. "That's the one. He does make money, I admit."

"What do we do now?"

"You wait here, by the scooter. I'll walk back for the other one."

She couldn't bear to be left alone. They walked back together, and he pulled a red scooter from a hedge and they rode it back along the road.

"Walk and ride, walk and ride," he said. "It's the only way. I want the two scooters back in the garage tonight where they belong."

"Couldn't I just *sit* on one?" she asked. It was such a pathetic admission, not being able to ride a scooter. "It's downhill all the way. If you show me the brake, I can ride it without the motor."

"Brains, mademoiselle, brains. This is the brake."

"Just like a bicycle!"

"The same. I'll ride behind you in case you fall off or need a push."

She had already decided to learn to ride a scooter. It was like typing or sewing, one of the small skills that everybody should take for granted. It galled her to roll to a halt on the flat and have to hand it over to Pennard to push uphill. The journey back to Saint-Tombe took over an hour, a distance that was only a ten-minute turn in a car. She waited furtively outside the yard while he wheeled both machines inside and locked them up.

"We must go to the police now," she whispered. "They can't have got far—that car's easy to recognize."

He drew her along the street, away from the yard.

"Now listen carefully, mademoiselle. You are not well, you've had a bad evening—"

"Not all the time."

"A full evening, nevertheless. You are too nervous to make decisions. You are prostrated with nerves. Trust me. Go home and go to bed. If your brother-in-law hasn't gone to the police, do nothing. Nothing at all. If he has, well, you are prostrated with nerves."

"But why?"

"Use your beautiful brains, mademoiselle. You have smuggled a fortune in diamonds into France, or you think you have. They were smuggled for your Monsieur Sevink. A man has been killed. Would you like to be arrested on suspicion?"

"But I'm innocent?"

"Your brother-in-law isn't. Will his wife like to see him in a prison far from home? Will you enjoy being found innocent after some months in jail?"

162

"My God!"

"Silence, therefore, mademoiselle."

"Yes, yes!"

"Goodnight, mademoiselle."

"Goodnight, monsieur. And thank you, monsieur." She took his hand in both of hers.

"I shall see you tomorrow."

"Yes, please. I'm still thinking of going home tomorrow."

"Very wise." The sound advice left a sad taste. She watched him turn and walk into the yard, and went home. Rosemary, of course, was waiting in the kitchen. Somehow the idea of having to make mundane explanations to a sister had never occurred to Helen.

"What the devil have you two been up to?" Rosemary demanded. "You fall and stun yourself, and Albert's got appendicitis all in the one night!"

"Appendicitis?" Helen looked at her blankly.

"Yes, appendicitis, if you please. Panic stations, cancel everything, home tomorrow, no French doctors for His Majesty, he's got to get home. Holiday scuppered, everything scuppered. What the hell's been going on?"

"I didn't realize Albert was feeling bad," Helen said weakly. "Are you really going home tomorrow?"

"He's got the damn plane booked and everything. He even tried to get a space for you—oh, when Albert goes home, everybody goes home. I told him to mind his own business and leave you alone, it's not *your* appendix."

Helen sat down at the table.

"Did he get me a booking?"

"No, he got the last one for our car, you'll have to wait till Friday—if you go. I never heard such nonsense in my life. Why can't he see a French doctor? We've hardly *got* here."

Ah, good old reliable Albert. Albert would never let you down.

"He's in bed," Rosemary added. "More alcoholic than appendicitic, if you ask me. I could kill him. And all that money down the drain! The rent of this place for a month, ta ta! He said, if you wanted, you could travel with us and have your car sent over later. Did you ever hear the like?"

"No, well . . . I'll stay and take care of the rent and so on," Helen offered. "And come home on Friday."

"Oh, Albert'll pay the full rent, don't worry. Oh, I see, you mean take care of it. You might as well stay out the month, if it comes to that. I'm about sick of the whole business. Some holiday!"

Helen succeeded in freeing herself eventually and getting to bed. There was an ugly black bruise below one knee, and her shins were decorated with scratches, but apart from fatigue, she felt unreasonably well. She lay in her bed without even wondering if the little red car was all right. Then she crossed her arms round herself and smiled slowly into the darkness and fell asleep.

13

THERE WAS NO SIGN OF PAUL PENNARD NEXT
day, but there was too much to do to leave any time for
worrying about him. The children were outraged at the prospect of being dragged home at the beginning of the holiday,
and Albert, bleary-eyed, was careful to walk uncomfortably
and rest a hand on his groin from time to time.

"Stop nattering!" he barked at Vanessa. "If the doctor says
it's not too serious when we get home, I'll take you on a boat
on the Norfolk Broads. A big boat."

"A speedboat?" Roddy asked.

"Sure, any damned kind of boat you damned well want."

"I would rather stay with Aunt Helen," Vanessa wailed. But
the thought of a speedboat was already working on her too.
The protest was automatic. Rosemary flew through the house
ramming clothes in suitcases and subjecting Albert to the
silence treatment. Every time he saw her he shrugged and
stooped over his appendix.

"Thank God you got home all right," he muttered to Helen.
"You looked pretty dicky after you fell. Was everything all
right?"

"Everything was just great, Albert." He cringed and walked
away clutching his appendix again.

"Are you sure you can manage?" he asked her, when the

Cresta was packed and the children were standing miserably around it, stealing the last few minutes.

"Helen can manage!" Rosemary snapped at him. "She's not a hypochondriac like some people! Just you keep the house for the month, Helen, it's paid for and I wouldn't give away a penny to these French landlords."

"I'll see."

"Sorry to muck up your holiday." Albert's eyes were pleading with her, and she tried to be pleasant for the sake of Rosemary.

"Accidents can happen," she said lightly. He didn't try to kiss her good-bye, and she was grateful, for Pennard walked into the courtyard at that moment. It was fantastic. He still looked like any French mechanic, a wiry brown-faced man in faded overalls. She refused to let her eyes linger on his face. What need? She could have closed her eyes and still have seen every plane, every line of his face. His eyes were bright blue. Astonishing.

"I came about the car, mademoiselle." He spoke in English. Probably rehearsed, Helen thought, and tried to stem a surge of affection that was almost maternal as she pictured him painstakingly going over the words. She was probably wrong. One was nearly always wrong in imagining the inner processes of other people. She hardly knew him. How absurd it was to be pondering like this, with a murder freshly committed. We have to disassociate or we would go insane, the psychological block. . . . She turned to him casually, groping for an answer that wouldn't sound insane, but Rosemary was already speaking.

"Not now, we're busy! We've got enough to worry about. Tomorrow, monsieur. . . ." She was waving her hand, doing the speech-to-a-deaf-idiot routine. "Too busy, O.K.?"

"Yes, I understand, madame. Later, perhaps." Pennard made a little polite gesture, turned and walked away. No, Helen thought, that one hadn't done any painstaking rehearsal. He was so damned self-contained that it was humiliating. He had come along out of a sense of politeness, or duty, but he wasn't bothered—he simply wasn't bothered. He walked away like any French mechanic, willing to work if required, otherwise not bothered at all.

"A bit too damned familiar, him, if you ask me," Rosemary was saying, and she looked closely at Helen. "I don't know if it's such a good idea, you staying for the month by yourself. These people impose on you, you know. Women on their own are fair game."

"Oh, for heaven's sake, Rosemary." Helen's impatience was genuine, and she hoped it sounded genuine.

"Don't be too sure." Albert momentarily forgot the agony of his appendix. She could sense that he was trying to speak between the lines. "We've got plenty of room, you could come with us still—somebody else could bring your car over. That guy, even—slip him a couple of quid and he would drive it to the airport and bung it aboard."

"I wouldn't trust any of them an inch!" Rosemary was torn as usual between trusting Helen to stay alone and trusting some foreigner with a new car.

"How about it, Helen?" Albert's voice was urgent. "No place like home, eh?"

"No." Helen's mind was made up. What was the sense of running away? That was sufficient reason for not leaving with Albert, without going into any other possible reasons. Rosemary shrugged her shoulders and told the children to get into the car. To Helen's astonishment, Roddy came to her to kiss her good-bye as well as Vanessa.

"Next year I'll swim as good as you!" he said, blushing.

"Okay, I'll race you next year," Helen said. She patted the bullet head and held Vanessa's hand. Albert got behind the wheel and tried to say something, but after a few seconds he breathed deeply and started up. She followed the car into the roadway and waved to the children as it shot away, far too fast, toward the east. She walked back into the house and tried to decide how she felt. Sudden loneliness made her feel private and glad to be alone. I was built for the solitary condition, she thought. At the same time, she felt more alone than she had for a long time. Families were an encumbrance, but they made a familiar human sound, and the contrast of silence was deafening. I must cure myself of analyzing my blasted feelings, always picking, picking, picking at myself. But she went on persuading herself that she was thinking about herself, and Rosemary and Albert, and she found that she was standing in the kitchen with her arms crossed and wrapped tightly round her, in an unconscious gesture that startled her, and had nothing to do with Albert and Rosemary, and her face grew hot. Good heavens, perhaps it showed—had Rosemary been showing mere sisterly suspicion, or had she seen something more specific, when she talked darkly about Pennard? No, she couldn't have known; on the outside nothing was different. Helen started to put her hands by her side and then snorted and said aloud, "Why should I? There's nobody here. . . ." She held herself tightly and laughed. This was what people meant by the old sordid story, the stray spinster and the married man. How glibly they dismissed it. Sordid? The word was without meaning. It was futile and it was finished, but the color of life would never be the same again. The whole world would always be sharper and luminous, no matter what. It was impossible to stay in the cool dark house. She found her sunglasses and a book and set off for the beach, not to read, to feel the caress of the sun and love it.

Jumeau the policeman passed her on his bicycle, and she noticed him only when he turned to stare at her. Her start of guilt was hardly more than a twist. How easy it must be, after all, to be a criminal. You shut your guilt from your mind and smile at policemen; your secret knowledge even makes it more enjoyable. She nodded and smiled. Jumeau tried to switch from cold suspicion and return the smile but had to jerk his head away as his front wheel wobbled. Helen lifted her face to the sun, still smiling.

In Paris, the sunshine struck through the clothes of Laurent, the ex-coalminer ex-safeblower, and he walked slowly to avoid a flushed, overheated look. His problem was a small and almost agreeable one, with no murderous tension attached to it. He didn't know how he was next going to support himself, and he had nothing left in the world but a few francs and an aging Citroën. The Citroën must be sold, that was certain, but nobody wanted an old Citroën in a hurry, with cash to pay for it, and he was combing deeper and deeper through his old acquaintances for a client. The latest on his list was old Gaston. He had drunk fairly regularly at Gaston's when he first came to Paris, and although he hadn't seen the old boy for a couple of years, Gaston was good-natured and well enough off, and he hadn't a car then. Even if he didn't want the Citroën, he might be good for a loan on the strength of it.

He was a little disappointed to find Gaston's wife behind the bar instead of the patron himself, but Laurent bought a glass of wine, and offered one to her, and made himself pleasant without seeming anxious. He bought a second glass. Still there was no sign of Gaston.

"How is Gaston?" he asked finally.

"Gaston! Gaston died a year ago! I thought you would know, monsieur," the widow said in reproach. She wiped her eyes with a corner of her apron in automatic grief.

"So healthy," Laurent muttered. "Gaston, of all people." He shook his head and tried to think of the next client on his list.

"You're a very bad man . . . Aristide?"

"Yes, Aristide."

"You're a very bad man, Aristide. A whole year, and you didn't know, it's so long since you deserted us. Ah, poor Gaston, he missed old friends."

"Eh, poor Gaston."

"None of the old crowd comes round these days," she said sadly. "It's very bad of you. Ah, it's a lonely life for a widow."

Laurent felt acutely uncomfortable.

"Be assured, madame, I shall make a point of coming regularly. Gaston was a good friend to me."

"Is that a promise?" There was always a hard business streak in these plump women. The place was probably running down without Gaston to be pleasant to the customers. Laurent nodded insincerely and decided that he would try to find Jules Lanvin. Jules always had some money about him.

"Would you like lunch, monsieur?"

He brought his attention back to the widow. He had no time to waste on lunch. The day was half gone. Ah, what the hell, he had to eat some time, he might as well be polite.

"Of course, madame," he said, "I was always crazy about your cooking, you know that."

"Oh, you men, flatterers every one. Well, you may as well come into the kitchen, after all you're more of an old friend than a customer." The glitter in her eye made Laurent's heart leap. Knowledge came to him that he and the widow had been conducting separate conversations and that hers was much the more interesting. That beady look of the widow's wasn't business . . . at least, not *business* business.

"Ah, I couldn't impose on your friendship," he said. She drew him a sidewise look and slapped his shoulder. Laurent shrugged and followed her into the kitchen. He tried not to rub his hands. He decided not to sell the Citroën.

Sevink felt better after he had had some sleep and meticulously posted the cash for the rent of the villa, with a noncommittal note mentioning pressure of business. He felt even better when he had made some complex but efficient arrangements to sell the Impala with its previous ownership neatly buried. But he decided he would feel even better some distance farther south than Paris. Italy, perhaps. He pondered the question of whether or not he should take Cabas and Savaron with him and decided in the end that he must. For the moment, he preferred to know where they were and what they were up to, and he had an uncomfortable fear that they might turn ugly if he tried to abandon them. They were such a silent pair of oafs. Their silence had always pleased him before. Now it irritated him immeasurably, especially the silence of Cabas. He was now convinced of Cabas' treachery, but a man who rarely spoke rarely revealed himself.

They set off from Paris in a Frégate, a sound but unobtrusive machine, with Cabas at the wheel. Sevink spent many miles staring at the back of Cabas' head and deliberating on how to trap him. The day was hot and the inactivity got on Sevink's nerves, which were less calm than usual after the business of the previous night. Eighty miles south, he burst out in a quite uncharacteristic anger against Cabas for taking a bend too fast. Cabas didn't even shrug. Sevink, white with anger, blurted out his accusation and leaned forward and grabbed Cabas' shoulder. The Frégate swerved so sharply that it glanced into the side of a coach traveling north with forty German tourists, and from there it bounced back and slewed across the road to fold itself round an apple tree, at one hundred kilometers per hour. The coach passengers fell about and shrieked but were not much hurt. The coach driver was absolutely livid.

A great weight was off Madame Robet's heart. Charles, dear foolish, irresponsible, ill Charles, had opened his eyes and spoken. Weakly, but quite rationally. Absolutely like himself, in fact. He had focused on her face as she sat by his bedside and said, "Aw, stop staring at me, for God's sake, Mother!" Then he fell into quite an easy sleep. Madame Robet, overcome with joy, tightened her lips grimly and looked stern and decided to remember later all the things she had promised to God. In the meantime, she could get on with her work. And there would never be a better opportunity of giving Charles' room a complete cleanout, when he was safely unconscious and couldn't nag her about prying into his things. He would spend hours over the clothes he was wearing and leave all the other things heaped on the floor. Prying! As if a boy had any real secrets from his mother. She knew what he was afraid of, that she would find the pathetic maga-

172

zines and pin-up pictures, and the photographs—as if he and his generation had invented that nasty nonsense for the first time. Men were like that, children, and Madame Robet knew all, all about it. She wouldn't destroy his silly toys.

She tidied a whole drawerful of the disagreeable things without doing more than wrinkle her nose, and when she came across some more precocious toys, she merely sighed and replaced them too. The boy was growing up, that was all. There was still a good, satisfying job of cleaning and emptying and straightening to be done without worrying about such nonsense. The child was like a magpie. He never threw anything away—broken catapults, a tattered old bonnet of feathers he had played Indians with as a little boy, forgotten birds' eggs and a mangled gyroscope, a toy speedboat that had never worked. And a whole boxful of marbles mixed up with his fancy cuff links. He would squeal if he saw her touching any of it, but he would never miss the rubbish if it was gone when he got up. She dropped all of the forgotten treasures into a cardboard box to throw away, and on a virtuous impulse, presented the lot to the twins next door. It cost nothing and might make them more respectful in future.

The twins were nine years old and not very imaginative. They liked the marbles at first because there were so many of them, but they were crude things, not properly round, more like pebbles than marbles. They filled their pockets with the things, and some time later, down at the beach, they used them as ammunition for the catapult that still worked, firing at a floating bottle bobbing well out from the rocks in the deep, deep water. When the supply of pebbles was finished, they searched the beach for others. Later the catapult broke, and they threw that in the water too. When Charles was able to get up and find the stones missing, he was haunted by the

173

nightmares of gangsters and policemen that had filled his coma, and never found the courage to ask if there had been burglars in the house. Madame Robet wasn't surprised that he never mentioned them. She had known all along that he wouldn't notice they were missing.

14 HELEN'S MIND WAS QUITE MADE UP. SHE
would book space on a plane on Friday, if there was any,
and go back home. It was out of the question to stay in Saint-
Tombe for the whole month. To her amazement, she couldn't
summon up any panic about a possible police investigation or
about Sevink. All that belonged to a dream that had vanished
with the daylight. But she would never be able to endure a
whole month of inaction; not in Saint-Tombe, at any rate,
where she would be a constant embarrassment to Paul Pennard. It would be too dreadful to meet his wife, too, and that
was bound to happen if she stayed so long. Then there was
the question of her own embarrassment, if she could feel that
he thought she was trying to . . . to hang on, if he got the
wrong impression. She was one spinster who had no illusions
and made no demands. She had no illusions and no regrets.
The thing was over and it must be tidily put away. She
would go home and wind up her own affairs and then be
really free to think of her next move. Canada, maybe. She
felt the need of some massive leap into a new situation where
she could begin as a new person. She *was* a new person. She
smiled, with the sun still hot on her face.

The little beach was still busy, and her eye was caught by
a family sitting in front of a bright orange tent with a table

and canvas chairs and a massive picnic basket and a portable radio. The mother was bulging from a rigidly boned
bathing suit and the father was dozing with mouth open and
plump limbs flopped out, like a starfish, and the three children
were sitting listlessly and whining for sweets. A French ver-
sion of Albert and Rosemary. She experienced an enormous
gratitude and superiority and was ashamed of it and glad.
There was a young couple frolicking in the water, not more
than seventeen or eighteen, the boy dark and tanned, in a
tiny bathing slip, the girl in a tinier scarlet bikini. Helen
watched them covertly with half-shut eyes, not wishing to
look like a peeper. They were leaping like dolphins and duck-
ing each other in the water, and there was just a shade of
something more than playfulness in their game, the boy's
hands always seemed to grab too shrewdly and hold on too
long, and the girl's face laughing into his was joyful and
innocent and secret, too, wrapped in conspiracy. Helen loved
them, without envy. I'm one of you, she would have said, if
there was any way in the world to say it.

She ate in the flashiest of the restaurants on the sea front
but couldn't bring herself to drink any wine because she was
alone. She concentrated on her book in order to preserve her
privacy and read the same page five times. She would read it
properly in the evenings. A quiet evening with a book was
what she needed. She would organize the house to get enough
light for reading comfortably, move all the beds if necessary.
She paid the bill and walked home, a slender girl with a
rather sallow complexion and a rather athletic stride and a
book dangling from one hand and a withdrawn, private smile.
An Englishman sitting at a table on the pavement beside his
beautiful and dark wife, who had a slender figure and a sallow complexion, unobtrusively moved his chair round so that

he could watch her with uninterested eyes until she disappeared.

Dusk fell very quickly. She was in the kitchen, feeling aimless, when there was a knock on the door, and she called out in faint alarm.

"It's me, mademoiselle. Pennard."

She opened the door, and he stood outside, in a dark jacket and a white shirt, until she stepped back and invited him in.

"Your relatives are away."

"Yes."

"I saw them going."

So he wasn't quite so self-contained; he had enough ordinary curiosity to have hung about and kept watch.

"A glass of wine, monsieur?"

"Thank you, you are very kind."

He had said that before, but that was before. She was glad to find that she could fall into a formality that was almost unembarrassed. But there was no wine. He nodded his head to vermouth, and she poured two glasses and sat opposite him at the kitchen table.

"I came about the car, mademoiselle."

"Yes. Well, it's very good of you, but what's the point now? I hope to go home on Friday." There was doubt in his face, and she added, "Oh, of course, the paint—if you've bought the paint for it, naturally I'll pay for it, monsieur. But there's no need to worry about it now, really."

"No, not the paint, mademoiselle. It's the question of this . . . secret compartment." She realized that he was trying not to look at her, and his embarrassment infected her. She stared into her glass.

"It's under the fender, on the right, mademoiselle. I looked for it while you were out. It's a question of suspicion, you understand. It would be inconvenient if a Customs official noticed it, even empty."

"Good Lord!" This had never occurred to her.

"You leave on Friday . . . still, it can be done. I propose to take the car into the garage and unfortunately drop something heavy—a stone, perhaps—on the fender. Then unfortunately I shall be obliged to do some work on the fender to repair the damage . . . fresh paint, that sort of thing."

Helen's breath exploded in a long whistle.

"Monsieur Pennard, you're a marvel, I would never have given it a thought. Could you really do it? I can't tell you how grateful I am. You are . . . most kind, monsieur." She blushed.

He shrugged and said, "Nothing, nothing."

"Have another glass?"

"Why not? If I'm not keeping you?"

"No, no, I'm not doing anything. I'm just . . ." What the hell did it matter what she was just doing? She fell silent and filled the glasses.

"And what will you do now, mademoiselle? I hope you will forget everything, especially the police."

"Yes, you were right about that, monsieur. It seems wrong, but I agree with you."

"Good. As I said, you are not hysterical."

They exchanged a small smile at that, a faint ghost of their intimacy.

"I think I may sell my house and go abroad," Helen said suddenly. "Canada, perhaps, I thought. I have nobody, you see—" and as she saw his questioning expression, she hastily added, "I mean, I am free to go wherever I like, I have no family. It's a good thing, to be free."

"No one at all?"

"No one." The liquor warmed and relaxed her. She found

herself telling him about her situation, about the years of tending an irascible spoiled father, teaching infants as a welcome relief from claustrophobia. He nodded from time to time without speaking. It was extraordinarily easy to talk to him, this ordinary French mechanic. Sympathetic quietness appeared to be fastened to him like a garment. She hoped fervently that his wife appreciated this quality.

"It sounds like a good idea," he said at last. "Go away, try something new. I sometimes think I might do the same."

"Monsieur Pennard," she said, "there's one thing I must say to you. I don't want to be a bore about this, but you don't know me very well, and I must explain this to you. . . . About our adventure, that's to say last night, you know what I mean . . . this was very pleasant, that's the only way I shall describe it, but now that it's no longer last night, well, last night is in the past, that's understood."

"Of course, mademoiselle."

"If I were hysterical . . ." she smiled. "I would wish you didn't agree quite so readily. But thank God, we understand each other, monsieur, we can be candid without embarrassment."

"It's a rare thing." Pennard smiled and lifted his glass to her, and she had the small satisfaction of a necessary job well done.

"I've thought of moving away myself," he said, half to himself. "America? No, not really. Perhaps somewhere else in France, Switzerland. A change, that's all."

"Wouldn't your . . . your family mind? I mean they agree?" It was a little sad that she wouldn't be able to think of him, in the future, in Saint-Tombe, that he would be vanished to some place without trace, even though it didn't matter in any practical sense.

179

"My family? Ah, that's my problem." His gesture dismissed his family, and Helen felt a fresh stab of curiosity about his wife.

"Well, good luck, monsieur."

"Thank you." They drank, and then there was nothing more to say. After a moment's hesitation, Pennard stood up, and Helen stood up with him.

"If you give me your keys," he said, "I'll take the car now and bring it back and leave it when I've finished."

"Yes, it's better that way."

So. Good-bye. All for the best. There was one little something unsaid, and Helen would always wonder how she had nearly not said it. He shook her hand, and she had her last chance to ease the load on her conscience.

"I hope, monsieur," she said quickly, "that this won't . . . won't affect anything . . . with your wife." He shrugged his shoulders.

"J'suis veuf."

"Yes, quite."

He turned to go.

"Pardon, monsieur?" she said.

"I am a widower, mademoiselle."

"I'm sorry."

"Thank you."

He turned to go again, and her voice stuck immovably in her throat. He walked across the courtyard into the darkness.

"Monsieur . . . a moment, please."

Pennard came back into the kitchen. His smile was slightly strained. He left the door open behind him. Helen wrung her hands, put one hand to her mouth and felt utterly silly.

"I'm sorry, monsieur, it's nothing really—it's only that I

took it for granted . . . that you had a wife. I shouldn't have called you back. . . ."

"Please don't worry, mademoiselle, be calm. We understand each other. You mustn't be afraid that because—because I am free . . . that I expect anything more of you."

"No, of course! I didn't mean that I expected anything of you either. I wouldn't want you to think that, monsieur. In fact, I'm glad to know that you are free . . . I mean, that I'm not on your conscience."

She looked wildly at him and tried to smile. Pennard's brow furrowed.

"Mademoiselle," he said, "let us have another glass of vermouth."

"Yes, oh yes, I'll get them, monsieur." But before they were poured, Pennard began to talk very quickly.

"Mademoiselle, if you go on Friday, you will go on Friday, that's fine, there's nothing to stop you. But I shall miss you."

"Very much?" She wheeled and spilled vermouth on the floor and ignored it.

"Very much. No, not very much, terribly, I'll miss you terribly. But you hardly know me, mademoiselle. What interest could you have in a garagiste? I'm not handsome, I'm not young, I'm not rich."

"Neither am I."

"You are, you are, beautiful and young and rich."

"Oh heavens!" She started to giggle. "This is insane. Would you marry me if I asked you, monsieur, a woman who is beautiful and young and rich?"

"You don't know me well enough to ask me to marry you, mademoiselle." His smile was so uncertain that her head swam. "I think I would have to say yes all the same," he said. "But this is foolishness when you don't know me."

"No, but we'll know each other better, monsieur."

"Paul?"

"Paul. Paul, I'm not impulsive, I would never decide my life without thinking. But anyway, you can spend the evening."

"Thank you." He beamed at her.

"I know," she babbled, "it's wonderful we can spend the evening like a married couple, I'll make some supper—I can cook. Eggs, eggs." She started to open cupboards and light the gas stove, a little hysterically.

"An omelette would please you?"

"Assuredly."

"Could you open this cupboard for me? It's stiff."

Pennard came forward and reached for the handle. Their hands touched and she closed her eyes and shuddered. His hand closed on her wrist, and his breathing sounded quick and heavy close to her ear.

"Monsieur," she said. "Paul, I mean. Why don't I make the omelette later?"

"Yes."

She turned clumsily and shamelessly and pressed herself against him. His arms moved, and he had picked her off the floor like a child. She kissed his eye by mistake.

"Through that door there," she said, and kissed his mouth.

"I wonder what became of the diamonds," she said.

"Pardon?"

"Nothing."

THE PERENNIAL LIBRARY MYSTERY SERIES

Delano Ames

CORPSE DIPLOMATIQUE   P 637, $2.84
"Sprightly and intelligent."
                              —*New York Herald Tribune Book Review*

FOR OLD CRIME'S SAKE   P 629, $2.84

MURDER, MAESTRO, PLEASE   P 630, $2.84
"If there is a more engaging couple in modern fiction than Jane and
Dagobert Brown, we have not met them."   —*Scotsman*

SHE SHALL HAVE MURDER   P 638, $2.84
"Combines the merit of both the English and American schools in the
new mystery. It's as breezy as the best of the American ones, and has
the sophistication and wit of any top-notch Britisher."
                              —*New York Herald Tribune Book Review*

E. C. Bentley

TRENT'S LAST CASE   P 440, $2.50
"One of the three best detective stories ever written."
                                              —Agatha Christie

TRENT'S OWN CASE   P 516, $2.25
"I won't waste time saying that the plot is sound and the detection
satisfying. Trent has not altered a scrap and reappears with all his old
humor and charm."   —Dorothy L. Sayers

Gavin Black

A DRAGON FOR CHRISTMAS   P 473, $1.95
"Potent excitement!"   —*New York Herald Tribune*

THE EYES AROUND ME   P 485, $1.95
"I stayed up until all hours last night reading *The Eyes Around Me*,
which is something I do not do very often, but I was so intrigued by the
ingeniousness of Mr. Black's plotting and the witty way in which he spins
his mystery. I can only say that I enjoyed the book enormously."
                                              —F. van Wyck Mason

YOU WANT TO DIE, JOHNNY?   P 472, $1.95
"Gavin Black doesn't just develop a pressure plot in suspense, he adds
uninfected wit, character, charm, and sharp knowledge of the Far East
to make rereading as keen as the first race-through."   —*Book Week*

Nicholas Blake

THE CORPSE IN THE SNOWMAN   P 427, $1.95
"If there is a distinction between the novel and the detective story (which we do not admit), then this book deserves a high place in both categories."   *—The New York Times*

THE DREADFUL HOLLOW   P 493, $1.95
"Pace unhurried, characters excellent, reasoning solid."
     —San Francisco Chronicle

END OF CHAPTER   P 397, $1.95
". . . admirably solid . . . an adroit formal detective puzzle backed up by firm characterization and a knowing picture of London publishing."   *—The New York Times*

HEAD OF A TRAVELER   P 398, $2.25
"Another grade A detective story of the right old jigsaw persuasion."
     —New York Herald Tribune Book Review

MINUTE FOR MURDER   P 419, $1.95
"An outstanding mystery novel. Mr. Blake's writing is a delight in itself."   *—The New York Times*

THE MORNING AFTER DEATH   P 520, $1.95
"One of Blake's best."   *—Rex Warner*

A PENKNIFE IN MY HEART   P 521, $2.25
"Style brilliant . . . and suspenseful."   *—San Francisco Chronicle*

THE PRIVATE WOUND   P 531, $2.25
[Blake's] best novel in a dozen years . . . . An intensely penetrating study of sexual passion. . . . A powerful story of murder and its aftermath."
     —Anthony Boucher, The New York Times

A QUESTION OF PROOF   P 494, $1.95
"The characters in this story are unusually well drawn, and the suspense is well sustained."   *—The New York Times*

THE SAD VARIETY   P 495, $2.25
"It is a stunner. I read it instead of eating, instead of sleeping."
     —Dorothy Salisbury Davis

THERE'S TROUBLE BREWING   P 569, $3.37
"Nigel Strangeways is a puzzling mixture of simplicity and penetration, but all the more real for that."   *—The Times Literary Supplement*

Nicholas Blake (cont'd)

THOU SHELL OF DEATH   P 428, $1.95
"It has all the virtues of culture, intelligence and sensibility that the most exacting connoisseur could ask of detective fiction."
—*The Times* [London] *Literary Supplement*

THE WIDOW'S CRUISE   P 399, $2.25
"A stirring suspense. . . . The thrilling tale leaves nothing to be desired."
—*Springfield Republican*

THE WORM OF DEATH   P 400, $2.25
"It [The Worm of Death] is one of Blake's very best—and his best is better than almost anyone's."
—Louis Untermeyer

John & Emery Bonett

A BANNER FOR PEGASUS   P 554, $2.40
"A gem! Beautifully plotted and set. . . . Not only is the murder adroit and deserved, and the detection competent, but the love story is charming."
—Jacques Barzun and Wendell Hertig Taylor

DEAD LION   P 563, $2.40
"A clever plot, authentic background and interesting characters highly recommended this one."
—*New Republic*

Christianna Brand

GREEN FOR DANGER   P 551, $2.50
"You have to reach for the greatest of Great Names (Christie, Carr, Queen . . .) to find Brand's rivals in the devious subtleties of the trade."
—Anthony Boucher

TOUR DE FORCE   P 572, $2.40
"Complete with traps for the over-ingenious, a double-reverse surprise ending and a key clue planted so fairly and obviously that you completely overlook it. If that's your idea of perfect entertainment, then seize at once upon *Tour de Force.*"
—Anthony Boucher, *The New York Times*

James Byrom

OR BE HE DEAD   P 585, $2.84
"A very original tale . . . Well written and steadily entertaining."
—Jacques Barzun & Wendell Hertig Taylor, *A Catalogue of Crime*

Henry Calvin

IT'S DIFFERENT ABROAD P 640, $2.84

"What is remarkable and delightful, Mr. Calvin imparts a flavor of satire to what he renovates and compels us to take straight."

—Jacques Barzun

Marjorie Carleton

VANISHED P 559, $2.40

"Exceptional . . . a minor triumph."
—Jacques Barzun and Wendell Hertig Taylor, *A Catalogue of Crime*

George Harmon Coxe

MURDER WITH PICTURES P 527, $2.25

"[Coxe] has hit the bull's-eye with his first shot."

—*The New York Times*

Edmund Crispin

BURIED FOR PLEASURE P 506, $2.50

"Absolute and unalloyed delight."

—Anthony Boucher, *The New York Times*

Lionel Davidson

THE MENORAH MEN P 592, $2.84

"Of his fellow thriller writers, only John Le Carré shows the same instinct for the viscera." —*Chicago Tribune*

NIGHT OF WENCESLAS P 595, $2.84

"A most ingenious thriller, so enriched with style, wit, and a sense of serious comedy that it all but transcends its kind."

—*The New Yorker*

THE ROSE OF TIBET P 593, $2.84

"I hadn't realized how much I missed the genuine Adventure story . . . until I read *The Rose of Tibet*." —Graham Greene

D. M. Devine

MY BROTHER'S KILLER P 558, $2.40

"A most enjoyable crime story which I enjoyed reading down to the last moment." —Agatha Christie

Kenneth Fearing

THE BIG CLOCK   P 500, $1.95

"It will be some time before chill-hungry clients meet again so rare a compound of irony, satire, and icy-fingered narrative. *The Big Clock* is . . . a psychothriller you won't put down."   —*Weekly Book Review*

Andrew Garve

THE ASHES OF LODA   P 430, $1.50

"Garve . . . embellishes a fine fast adventure story with a more credible picture of the U.S.S.R. than is offered in most thrillers."

       —*The New York Times Book Review*

THE CUCKOO LINE AFFAIR   P 451, $1.95

". . . an agreeable and ingenious piece of work."   —*The New Yorker*

A HERO FOR LEANDA   P 429, $1.50

"One can trust Mr. Garve to put a fresh twist to any situation, and the ending is really a lovely surprise."   —*The Manchester Guardian*

MURDER THROUGH THE LOOKING GLASS   P 449, $1.95

". . . refreshingly out-of-the-way and enjoyable . . . highly recommended to all comers."   —*Saturday Review*

NO TEARS FOR HILDA   P 441, $1.95

"It starts fine and finishes finer. I got behind on breathing watching Max get not only his man but his woman, too."   —*Rex Stout*

THE RIDDLE OF SAMSON   P 450, $1.95

"The story is an excellent one, the people are quite likable, and the writing is superior."   —*Springfield Republican*

Michael Gilbert

BLOOD AND JUDGMENT   P 446, $1.95

"Gilbert readers need scarcely be told that the characters all come alive at first sight, and that his surpassing talent for narration enhances any plot. . . . Don't miss."   —*San Francisco Chronicle*

THE BODY OF A GIRL   P 459, $1.95

"Does what a good mystery should do: open up into all kinds of ramifications, with untold menace behind the action. At the end, there is a bang-up climax, and it is a pleasure to see how skilfully Gilbert wraps everything up."   —*The New York Times Book Review*

Michael Gilbert (cont'd)

THE DANGER WITHIN P 448, $1.95

"Michael Gilbert has nicely combined some elements of the straight detective story with plenty of action, suspense, and adventure, to produce a superior thriller." —*Saturday Review*

FEAR TO TREAD P 458, $1.95

"Merits serious consideration as a work of art."

—*The New York Times*

Joe Gores

HAMMETT P 631, $2.84

"Joe Gores at his very best. Terse, powerful writing—with the master, Dashiell Hammett, as the protagonist in a novel I think he would have been proud to call his own." —*Robert Ludlum*

C. W. Grafton

BEYOND A REASONABLE DOUBT P 519, $1.95

"A very ingenious tale of murder . . . a brilliant and gripping narrative." —*Jacques Barzun and Wendell Hertig Taylor*

THE RAT BEGAN TO GNAW THE ROPE P 639, $2.84

"Fast, humorous story with flashes of brilliance."

—*The New Yorker*

Edward Grierson

THE SECOND MAN P 528, $2.25

"One of the best trial-testimony books to have come along in quite a while." —*The New Yorker*

Bruce Hamilton

TOO MUCH OF WATER P 635, $2.84

"A superb sea mystery. . . . The prose is excellent."
—*Jacques Barzun and Wendell Hertig Taylor, A Catalogue of Crime*

Cyril Hare

DEATH IS NO SPORTSMAN P 555, $2.40

"You will be thrilled because it succeeds in placing an ingenious story in a new and refreshing setting. . . . The identity of the murderer is really a surprise." —*Daily Mirror*

DEATH WALKS THE WOODS   P 556, $2.40

"Here is a fine formal detective story, with a technically brilliant solution demanding the attention of all connoisseurs of construction."

　　　　—Anthony Boucher, *The New York Times Book Review*

AN ENGLISH MURDER   P 455, $2.50

"By a long shot, the best crime story I have read for a long time. Everything is traditional, but originality does not suffer. The setting is perfect. Full marks to Mr. Hare."　　　　　—*Irish Press*

SUICIDE EXCEPTED   P 636, $2.84

"Adroit in its manipulation . . . and distinguished by a plot-twister which I'll wager Christie wishes she'd thought of."

　　　　—*The New York Times*

TENANT FOR DEATH   P 570, $2.84

"The way in which an air of probability is combined both with clear, terse narrative and with a good deal of subtle suburban atmosphere, proves the extreme skill of the writer."　　　　—*The Spectator*

TRAGEDY AT LAW   P 522, $2.25

"An extremely urbane and well-written detective story."

　　　　—*The New York Times*

UNTIMELY DEATH   P 514, $2.25

"The English detective story at its quiet best, meticulously underplayed, rich in perceivings of the droll human animal and ready at the last with a neat surprise which has been there all the while had we but wits to see it."　　　　—*New York Herald Tribune Book Review*

THE WIND BLOWS DEATH   P 589, $2.84

"A plot compounded of musical knowledge, a Dickens allusion, and a subtle point in law is related with delightfully unobtrusive wit, warmth, and style."　　　　—*The New York Times*

WITH A BARE BODKIN   P 523, $2.25

"One of the best detective stories published for a long time."

　　　　—*The Spectator*

Robert Harling

THE ENORMOUS SHADOW   P 545, $2.50

"In some ways the best spy story of the modern period. . . . The writing is terse and vivid . . . the ending full of action . . . altogether first-rate."

—Jacques Barzun and Wendell Hertig Taylor, *A Catalogue of Crime*

Matthew Head

THE CABINDA AFFAIR   P 541, $2.25
"An absorbing whodunit and a distinguished novel of atmosphere."
                    —Anthony Boucher, *The New York Times*

THE CONGO VENUS   P 597, $2.84
"Terrific. The dialogue is just plain wonderful."
                    —*The Boston Globe*

MURDER AT THE FLEA CLUB   P 542, $2.50
"The true delight is in Head's style, its limpid ease combined with humor
and an awesome precision of phrase."   —*San Francisco Chronicle*

M. V. Heberden

ENGAGED TO MURDER   P 533, $2.25
"Smooth plotting."
                    —*The New York Times*

James Hilton

WAS IT MURDER?   P 501, $1.95
"The story is well planned and well written."
                    —*The New York Times*

P. M. Hubbard

HIGH TIDE   P 571, $2.40
"A smooth elaboration of mounting horror and danger."
                    —*Library Journal*

Elspeth Huxley

THE AFRICAN POISON MURDERS   P 540, $2.25
"Obscure venom, manical mutilations, deadly bush fire, thrilling climax
compose major opus.... Top-flight."
                    —*Saturday Review of Literature*

MURDER ON SAFARI   P 587, $2.84
"Right now we'd call Mrs. Huxley a dangerous rival to Agatha Christie."
                    —*Books*

Mary Kelly

THE SPOILT KILL P 565, $2.40

"Mary Kelly is a new Dorothy Sayers. . . . [An] exciting new novel."
—*Evening News*

Lange Lewis

THE BIRTHDAY MURDER P 518, $1.95

"Almost perfect in its playlike purity and delightful prose."
—Jacques Barzun and Wendell Hertig Taylor

Allan MacKinnon

HOUSE OF DARKNESS P 582, $2.84

"His best . . . a perfect compendium."
—Jacques Barzun & Wendell Hertig Taylor, *A Catalogue of Crime*

Arthur Maling

LUCKY DEVIL P 482, $1.95

"The plot unravels at a fast clip, the writing is breezy and Maling's approach is as fresh as today's stockmarket quotes."
—*Louisville Courier Journal*

RIPOFF P 483, $1.95

"A swiftly paced story of today's big business is larded with intrigue as a Ralph Nader-type investigates an insurance scandal and is soon on the run from a hired gun and his brother. . . . Engrossing and credible."
—*Booklist*

SCHROEDER'S GAME P 484, $1.95

"As the title indicates, this Schroeder is up to something, and the unravelling of his game is a diverting and sufficiently blood-soaked entertainment."
—*The New Yorker*

Austin Ripley

MINUTE MYSTERIES P 387, $2.50

More than one hundred of the world's shortest detective stories. Only one possible solution to each case!

Thomas Sterling

THE EVIL OF THE DAY P 529, $2.50

"Prose as witty and subtle as it is sharp and clear. . .characters unconventionally conceived and richly bodied forth . . . . In short, a novel to be treasured."
—Anthony Boucher, *The New York Times*

Julian Symons

THE BELTING INHERITANCE   P 468, $1.95
"A superb whodunit in the best tradition of the detective story."
                                        —August Derleth, *Madison Capital Times*

BLAND BEGINNING   P 469, $1.95
"Mr. Symons displays a deft storytelling skill, a quiet and literate wit,
a nice feeling for character, and detectival ingenuity of a high order."
                                        —Anthony Boucher, *The New York Times*

BOGUE'S FORTUNE   P 481, $1.95
"There's a touch of the old sardonic humour, and more than a touch of
style."   —*The Spectator*

THE BROKEN PENNY   P 480, $1.95
"The most exciting, astonishing and believable spy story to appear in
years.   —Anthony Boucher, *The New York Times Book Review*

THE COLOR OF MURDER   P 461, $1.95
"A singularly unostentatious and memorably brilliant detective story."
                                        —*New York Herald Tribune Book Review*

Dorothy Stockbridge Tillet
(John Stephen Strange)

THE MAN WHO KILLED FORTESCUE   P 536, $2.25
"Better than average."   —*Saturday Review of Literature*

Simon Troy

THE ROAD TO RHUINE   P 583, $2.84
"Unusual and agreeably told."   —*San Francisco Chronicle*

SWIFT TO ITS CLOSE   P 546, $2.40
"A nicely literate British mystery . . . the atmosphere and the plot are
exceptionally well wrought, the dialogue excellent."   —*Best Sellers*

Henry Wade

THE DUKE OF YORK'S STEPS   P 588, $2.84
"A classic of the golden age."
   —Jacques Barzun & Wendell Hertig Taylor, *A Catalogue of Crime*

A DYING FALL   P 543, $2.50
"One of those expert British suspense jobs . . . it crackles with undercur-
rents of blackmail, violent passion and murder. Topnotch in its class."
                                        —*Time*

THE HANGING CAPTAIN P 548, $2.50

"This is a detective story for connoisseurs, for those who value clear thinking and good writing above mere ingenuity and easy thrills."

—*Times Literary Supplement*

Hillary Waugh

LAST SEEN WEARING . . . P 552, $2.40

"A brilliant tour de force." —Julian Symons

THE MISSING MAN P 553, $2.40

"The quiet detailed police work of Chief Fred C. Fellows, Stockford, Conn., is at its best in *The Missing Man* . . . one of the Chief's toughest cases and one of the best handled."

—Anthony Boucher, *The New York Times Book Review*

Henry Kitchell Webster

WHO IS THE NEXT? P 539, $2.25

"A double murder, private-plane piloting, a neat impersonation, and a delicate courtship are adroitly combined by a writer who knows how to use the language." —Jacques Barzun and Wendell Hertig Taylor

Anna Mary Wells

MURDERER'S CHOICE P 534, $2.50

"Good writing, ample action, and excellent character work."

—*Saturday Review of Literature*

A TALENT FOR MURDER P 535, $2.25

"The discovery of the villain is a decided shock." —*Books*

Edward Young

THE FIFTH PASSENGER P 544, $2.25

"Clever and adroit . . . excellent thriller . . ." —*Library Journal*

If you enjoyed this book you'll want to know about
THE PERENNIAL LIBRARY MYSTERY SERIES
Buy them at your local bookstore or use this coupon for ordering:

Qty	P number	Price
———	———	———
———	———	———
———	———	———
———	———	———
———	———	———
———	———	———
———	———	———
———	———	———
———	———	———
———	———	———
———	———	———

postage and handling charge	$1.00
——— book(s) @ $0.25	———
TOTAL	

Prices contained in this coupon are Harper & Row invoice prices only.
They are subject to change without notice, and in no way reflect the prices at
which these books may be sold by other suppliers.

**HARPER & ROW, Mail Order Dept. #PMS, 10 East 53rd St., New
York, N.Y. 10022.**
Please send me the books I have checked above. I am enclosing $———
which includes a postage and handling charge of $1.00 for the first book and
25¢ for each additional book. Send check or money order. No cash or
C.O.D.s please

Name————————————————————————

Address—————————————————————————

City——————— State——————— Zip———————
Please allow 4 weeks for delivery. USA only. This offer expires 4/30/84
Please add applicable sales tax.